The Dinner Guest

GABRIELA YBARRA

The Dinner Guest

Translated from the Spanish by Natasha Wimmer

Harvill *Secker*
LONDON

1 3 5 7 9 10 8 6 4 2

Harvill Secker, an imprint of Vintage,
20 Vauxhall Bridge Road,
London SW1V 2SA

Harvill Secker is part of the Penguin Random House group of companies
whose addresses can be found at global.penguinrandomhouse.com

Penguin
Random House
UK

First published by Harvill Secker in 2018
First published with the title *El comensal* in Spain by Caballo de Troya,
Penguin Random House Grupo Editorial in 2015

A CIP catalogue record for this book is available from the British Library

penguin.co.uk/vintage

ISBN 9781910701980

Typeset in India by Integra Software Services Pvt. Ltd, Pondicherry

Printed and bound in Great Britain by Clays Ltd, St Ives plc

Penguin Random House is committed to a sustainable future
for our business, our readers and our planet. This book is
made from Forest Stewardship Council® certified paper.

For Ernestina, Enrique, Inés and Leticia

Who has beheld without trembling
a stand of beeches in a pinewood?

ANTONIO MACHADO

Author's Note

This novel is a free reconstruction of the story of my family, especially the first part, which takes place in the Basque Country in the spring of 1977, six years before I was born. During the months of May and June of that year, my father's father — my grandfather Javier — was kidnapped and killed. I heard the story for the first time when I was eight. A school friend, a grandson of the prosecutor on the case, explained to me how his grandfather had fished my grandfather's body out of the Nervión estuary with a trawl net, the kind that Galicians use to catch anchovies. Years later, the granddaughter of a medical examiner, a classmate at another school, told me that her grandfather had dissected my grandfather's body after it was discovered bound hand and foot and run over by a train near Larrabasterra station. For many years I took both stories to be true, and I mixed them with conversations overheard at home to make up a version of my own. But in July 2012 I felt the need to go deeper into the details of the killing of my grandfather. My mother had died almost a year before, and with her illness my father had begun to talk about death in a strange way. I suspected that the kidnapping had something to do with it. I googled my grandfather's name and visited archives. I took many notes on what I read, faithfully transcribing news stories and opinion pieces. But the scenes that I imagined ended up filtering into my account. What I describe in the following pages isn't an exact reconstruction of my grandfather's kidnapping or of what really happened to my family before, during and after my mother's illness: the names of some characters have been changed and some passages are inventions based on stories. Often, imagining has been the only way I've had to try to understand.

ONE

I

The story goes that in my family there's an extra dinner guest at every meal. He's invisible, but always there. He has a plate, glass, knife and fork. Every so often he appears, casts his shadow over the table and erases one of those present.

The first to vanish was my grandfather.

The morning of 20 May, 1977, Marcelina put a kettle on the stove. While she was waiting for it to come to the boil, she took a feather duster and began to dust the china. Upstairs, my grandfather was getting into the shower, and at the end of the hallway, where the doors made a U, the three siblings who still lived at home were in bed. My father didn't live there anymore, but on his way elsewhere from New York he had decided to come to Neguri to spend a few days with the family.

When the bell rang, Marcelina was far from the door. As she ran the feather duster over a Chinese vase she heard someone calling from the street: 'There's been an accident, open up!' and she ran to the kitchen. She glanced for a second at the kettle, which had begun to whistle, and slid the bolt without looking through the peephole. On the doorstep, four hooded attendants opened their coats to reveal machine guns.

'Where is Don Javier?' asked one. He pointed a gun at the girl, obliging her to show them the way to my grandfather. Two men and a woman went up the stairs. The third man stayed below, watching the front door and rifling through papers.

My father woke when he felt something cold graze his leg. He opened his eyes and saw a man raising the sheet with the barrel of a gun. From across the room, a woman repeated that he should relax, no one was going to hurt him. Then she moved slowly towards the bed, took his wrists and handcuffed them to the headboard. The man and the woman left the room, leaving my father alone, manacled, his torso bare and his face turned upward.

Thirty seconds went by, a minute, maybe longer. After a while, the hooded figures came back into the room. But this time they weren't alone; with them were two of my father's brothers and his youngest sister.

My grandfather was still in the shower when he heard someone shouting and banging on the door. He turned off the water, and when the noise didn't stop, he wrapped himself in a towel and poked his head out the door to see what was going on. A masked man had Marcelina under his arm; with his other hand he held the machine gun pointing through the open door. The man came into the bathroom and sat on the toilet. He grabbed the maid by the skirt and forced her to kneel in a puddle on the floor. Just inches away, my grandfather tried to comb his hair, his eyes on the gun reflected in the mirror. He put on hair cream, but his fingers were shaking and he couldn't make a straight parting. When he was done he came out of the bathroom and collected a rosary, his glasses, an inhaler and his missal. He knotted his tie, and with the machine gun at his back he walked to the bedroom where his children were.

The four of them were waiting on the bed, watching the woman who had Marcelina by the wrists. In the silence, the whistle of the kettle could be heard.

When she was done securing the maid, the woman went down to the kitchen, set the kettle on the counter and turned off the stove. Meanwhile, on the floor above, her companions shifted the captives. First they made them move to the ends of the bed, leaving a space. Then they pulled off my grandfather's tie and sat him in the middle.

The biggest man took a camera out of the black leather bag at his waist and pulled the ski mask out of the way to look through the viewfinder, but neither my father nor his siblings nor my grandfather looked at him. The hooded man snapped his fingers a few times to get their attention, and when he finally succeeded he pressed the shutter three times.

*

A point that has yet to be cleared up is the whereabouts of the photographs that the kidnappers took of the family, and the three snapshots of Ybarra that they removed from the house.

'I can confirm that we haven't received any of the three pictures of my father as evidence,' stated one of the children. 'We don't know what might have happened to them, or to the photographs that were taken of the family with my father moments before he was carried off. The photographs are of those of us who were at home at the time, together with him, saying our goodbyes.'

El País, Friday, 24 June, 1977

*

Mount Serantes was covered by a dense, heavy fog that broke up into heavy rain. Torrents poured down the mountainside into the Nervión estuary, which filled up gradually, like a bathtub. Its banks didn't overflow, but the banks of the Gobela, a river very near my grandfather's house, did. On Avenida de los Chopos the water spilled into the street, covered the pavements and surged into garages. Some cars' headlights came on by themselves. From inside the house the sound of the rain was loud, like someone throwing bread crusts at the windows. Outside, a number of roads were cut off: Bilbao-Santander near Retuerto, Neguri-Bilbao along the valley of Asúa, and Neguri-Algorta.

Beginning at 8.15 in the morning, cars piled up on the roads into Bilbao, in an 18-kilometre traffic jam that reached as far as Getxo. All over Vizcaya, the rain, the cars and the slap of wipers on windscreens could be heard. My grandfather was shut in the trunk of a SEAT 124D sedan making a slow getaway. In the front were two of the kidnappers, with the radio on. No one knew anything yet. 'Y te amaré', by Ana y Johnny, could still be heard between traffic and news breaks.

*

The articles from the days that followed the kidnapping are sketchy and brief. The first in-depth report I find was published on 25 May, 1977, in *Blanco y Negro*, a supplement of the newspaper *ABC*. It's titled 'The Worst They Can Do Is Shoot Me'. A few lines below, a column heading reads: 'Handcuffs French-Made'.

*

When my father trod in the puddles in the garden, he hadn't yet managed to get the handcuffs off. Upon reaching the gate, he pushed it open with his shoulder and stepped out. Water was rushing over the paving stones. My father scrutinized the street, the lamp post, the bushes, and the soaked hair of a woman loaded with shopping bags who stopped to his left. The woman put the bags on the ground to cover her head and said hello. He answered politely but briefly and walked on, getting wet, until he stopped in front of a house with stone walls, and hedges whipping between the rails of the fence. He rang the bell. He said: 'Hello, I live next door. Can I use the phone?' There was a buzz, the door quivered, and a maid with her hair in a bun asked him to come in. She led him into the house, stopped in front of a bone-coloured telephone on the wall and handed him the receiver. When she saw the handcuffs her mouth went a funny shape and she crossed herself. My father, dripping, dialled the police quickly without looking at her. He gave his first name, his last name, his location and a summary of what had happened that morning. Then he was silent, listening to the officer. The maid's eyes popped, as round as her bun. My father, though, looked calm.

*

Before leaving, the intruders warned my father and his siblings that they couldn't report the kidnapping until midday. At a quarter to twelve, two of the brothers managed to pull free of the bed frame. At twelve thirty the police arrived, followed fifteen minutes later by the press.

The officers freed the women first. Last was my youngest uncle, who, once he was released, ran down to the garden to shout my grandfather's name among the hydrangeas. My father spoke to the reporters on the porch. They stuck their tape recorders under his chin and he said, 'Everyone behaved impeccably. We were calm throughout it all.'

As the lunch hour neared, more policemen and reporters came. The rest of the siblings and some cousins arrived too. The oldest brother gazed down the road. Meanwhile, the youngest was still in the garden looking for my grandfather in the hydrangeas.

*

The oldest had blue eyes and was wearing a green anorak and jeans. The second, dark and thin, was wearing a dark checked shirt. The woman, slim, was wearing an orange raincoat. The fourth, of medium height, never took off his white coat. The four assailants ranged in age from twenty to twenty-five.

Blanco y Negro, Wednesday, May 25, 1977

*

Here are two pictures of my father in the aluminium handcuffs made by a French company, Peripedose.

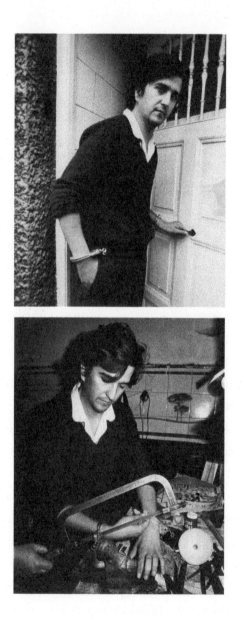

II

The wind came in the back door, circling the burners of the stove and knocking at the windows. The air on one side of the glass thumped against the air on the other side. The guests had gone and everyone who was left gathered in the living room, taking stock of the situation. On the floor, books and family photographs were still scattered; a bronze frame lay empty, and the wind cavorted at will, ruffling the fringe of the rug and making little tornados over the sofa.

The sawn-off handcuffs were sitting on the chest of drawers in the hall. Next to them were four lengths of rope, and the scraps of cotton with which the kidnappers had wrapped the women's wrists so as not to hurt them. The strips of tape for their mouths and the cloths used to cover their faces were in the bin in the kitchen. None of the siblings wanted to sleep alone in their rooms. They chose to lie down together, sprawled on the sofa.

Since the police had left, no one had returned to the back room. It upset my father and his siblings to remember the brass bars of the bed to which they had been bound. They were also haunted by the voices of the kidnappers, echoing soft and polite in their heads, the musical, bell-like *Don Javier* with which their captors had addressed my grandfather, never lowering their machine guns.

The siblings spent the day after the kidnapping in the living room of the house where the crime had been committed. The oldest brother stroked his chin. The youngest played at putting on and taking off his shoes with a nudge of the finger. On the table by the door there was a telephone that rang incessantly. A sibling exclaimed and took the receiver off the hook, leaving it on the tabletop. The noise ceased. Those present gathered around the sofa for protection from the silence.

Time passed, night fell and still there was no information about my grandfather. My father and his siblings paced the room. They moved to and from the sofa, clustered around it, leaned on it, stood. On the coffee table the radio was on, waiting for the news. The announcer began to speak precisely at ten, but there was no update on the kidnapping or my grandfather.

*

Outside the house nothing seemed to be happening, but a closer look would have revealed two Guardia Civil officers sitting in jeeps parked by the gate. The headlights and engines of the jeeps were turned off, but every half hour the drivers started their engines and cruised the streets around the house: down Avenida de los Chopos and Carretera de la Avanzada, along the Gobela river, and past the church of El Carmen. At four in the morning the streets were empty and no light showed in the windows of the house. Inside, no one was asleep; the siblings lay there awake in the dark, listening to one another's breathing.

My father got up from the sofa, opened the balcony door and went out to smoke a cigarette. It had stopped raining, but there were still drops of water on the railings. Inside the house, the memory of my grandfather was suffocating; recurring images of the kidnapping. But outside there was a breeze and he could think about the leaks at his apartment in Harlem, or about a bombed-out building he had visited in the Bronx. He extinguished his cigarette in the plumpest drop of water on the ledge and left the stub in a flower pot. He remembered he had to pick up some rolls of film from a lab in the centre of Bilbao. Then he looked out at the garden and thought about all the things he wanted to do when the kidnapping was over. He lit another cigarette and smoked it with his gaze on the branches of a chestnut tree.

At eleven thirty in the morning on Sunday, 22 May, an anonymous voice, feminine and fragile as a baby bird, called the Radio Popular broadcasting station: 'We've got Javier Ybarra,' it said, stumbling over the words. In the background, cars and the shouts of children could be heard. 'Check the mailbox in front of Number 37, Calle Urbieta in San Sebastián,' the voice said before hanging up.

The postman didn't like this particular mailbox, because every time he opened it, the rusty hinges squealed like a rodent. The mailbox was old. The rain had made channels between the bald patches where the paint was worn off, and now an enormous stain covered its domed top.

The document turned up in the spot indicated, in parts. First one typed sheet, then another, and finally the third. They hadn't been stapled or clipped together. The statement was unusually long, and written in a way that made it seem fake: there was no clear acknowledgement of the kidnapping or conditions for return. The postman, accompanied by a policeman, found only typewritten musings that left no opening for negotiation.

Meanwhile, my father and his siblings were still shut up in the house on Avenida de los Chopos, waiting for news, receiving the press and trying to communicate with the kidnappers. Around three in the morning, the oldest came into the living room, arm in arm with his wife. No one was sleeping. 'They want a billion pesetas,' he said, and tossed a bundle of bills on the table. The siblings spent all night counting money. The sum the kidnappers were demanding was impossible. When morning came, the older siblings made the rounds of the banks to see about a loan. The rest stayed home, pacing the living room and talking to reporters: 'It's a lie that they're asking for a billion pesetas,' said one of my uncles to the press. 'How did your father react last Friday?' asked one reporter. 'He showed no qualms about being kidnapped, not for a second. He got dressed, collected his hat and some books, and tried to reassure us,' said my father.

III

It isn't true that my grandfather's house was called Los Nardos. It was called Bidarte, or Crossroads, because it stood at an intersection.

It isn't true that my grandfather asked the kidnappers to kill him on the spot. What my grandfather said was: 'The worst you can do is shoot me.'

It isn't true that my father's youngest sister escaped the kidnappers by hiding in a wardrobe. She was bound to the bed frame, like everyone else.

Nor is it true that my father and his siblings began negotiations with the kidnappers that very Friday, 20 May.

*

On 31 May, 1977, a letter postmarked Bilbao appeared in the mailbox of a juvenile detention centre in Amurrio, in the province of Álava. The envelope had no return address and bulged strangely. Inside was a note written by my grandfather, which began: 'My dear children, at last my kidnappers have permitted me to write to you.' The text was handwritten in blue pen on a sheet of graph paper torn from a notebook. My grandfather's handwriting was steady, like his faith. In the letter he wrote that he was in good health and that he felt closer to God in his adversity: 'I fully accept whatever He has in store for me.' The mysterious object accompanying the note was the key that opened the communion box in his chapel at home.

Maybe my grandfather kept his savings in the box, or beneath a false bottom, so as not to mix money with God. Or maybe the key didn't belong to the box, but to a common cupboard, or a safe hidden behind a painting. Or maybe what he kept in the box wasn't money, but something of use to the kidnappers or their victim.

'Communion wafers have to be replaced,' said a sibling to the press. 'It's only natural for my father to worry about them and send us the key to the box. There really is no hidden message here. Receiving this letter has been a great comfort to us.' 'Also,' he went on, waving one hand, 'I get the sense that the kidnappers are treating him well, though of course I don't have much evidence to go on.'

*

The negotiations advanced in secret, and only rumours appeared in the papers. According to one, the siblings had made an offer of one hundred million pesetas, but the kidnappers had rejected it as ridiculous. According to another, my grandfather's captors would be satisfied with five hundred million. The family's silence was absolute: 'We can't provide any statement confirming or denying anything,' they said. A close relative told the press: 'Two hundred million – I doubt they'll be able to raise more than that.'

IV

The mud was up to the door handles. On 1 June, the police were notified that a SEAT 124D with the licence plate BI-6079-H had been abandoned in the middle of a boggy field high on Mount Artxanda. The forest road that climbed to the summit was full of puddles, branches, beech leaves and pine needles. The car was found at the bottom of a ditch, surrounded by trees and buried halfway up the wheels. In the glove compartment, the police found the registration papers and discovered that the vehicle was the property of the branch of a rental agency near Plaza de Campuzano, in the centre of Bilbao. The two officers knotted yellow plastic ties around tree trunks to cordon off the road. When they were done securing the area, one of the men put a roll of film in his camera and began to photograph the car and all the objects that he found inside it, including a special screwdriver that could be used to pick locks. As was later revealed, the vehicle had been rented on 17 May by a young man in his late twenties carrying a fake ID. The ID holder's initials were A.M.C.

The police hooked the car up to a tow truck and took it to a council parking garage in Bilbao. From the heights of Artxanda one could see Mount Pagasarri.

In the following days, the motorway checkpoints and searches intensified. The key areas were Artxanda, Enekuri, Algorta and the road from Bilbao to San Sebastián. New checkpoints were erected in Erletxes, San Ignacio and Leioa, and new searches were carried out in Gernika and Amurrio.

*

On 10 June, the second letter arrived, appearing in the mailbox at my grandfather's house on Avenida de los Chopos. The envelope was postmarked Bilbao, Monday, 6 June, and the text was dated Saturday, 4 June. The media published an abridged version; my father and his siblings decided to reserve any content that they deemed private. The published note read as follows:

My Dear Children,

Once again I'm able to write to you and I do so after receiving news of you and much else from the papers.

I'm sorry to be the cause of such trouble and I appreciate the interest that people and organisations have shown in the difficult situation in which I find myself.

In my solitude I have sought refuge in prayer, and the two books I brought with me have been of much assistance. Let us trust in the Holy Family, to which, as you well know, my devotion is great, in the belief that everything will surely be resolved for the good of our souls.

Don't worry about me, I'm in God's hands, I forgive those who have caused me offence and I ask forgiveness of anyone

I may have caused offence, and I offer my life up for the conversion of sinners and for the reunion of souls with the Divine Redeemer.

All my love, and may God bless and keep you,

your father,

Javier

*

The reporters questioned my father's oldest brother and his answers were nearly all evasive: 'Please understand, we can't say anything, I'm sorry, I can neither confirm nor deny anything.' Though I haven't read the whole letter, I know that the content that was withheld from the media consisted of commissions for the older siblings and advice for the adolescents.

The same evening that the siblings received the note, the kidnappers sent a message to Radio Popular's Bilbao broadcasting station in which they pressed the siblings to pay the ransom: 'The life of Javier de Ybarra rests in his family's hands, it's all up to them,' they said. 'The deadline for delivering the money is Saturday, 18 June, at 3 p.m.'

*

The older siblings paced in circles around the living room and called the go-between who was negotiating the ransom. My father reread the letter from my grandfather next to the window. 'The newspapers,' he said twice, loudly. At a nearby table, the siblings composed the following note:

Neguri, 11 June, 1977

Dear Father,

Yesterday we received your second letter, dated 4 June. It filled us with great joy to see, by what you write, that you have found spiritual comfort and strength, and that your whole family, your friends, your colleagues, and all those who make their home with you or made their home with our dear mother are very much present in your thoughts.

We want you to know that we have carried out the commissions with which you entrusted us, and that we are relying upon the solid Christian principles that you have always inculcated in us.

With deepest affection, in hopes of having you back among us soon, your loving children.

V

The priest took off his collar and buttoned a khaki shirt with roomy pockets. He went out. He stopped at a bar in the district of Abando and had an espresso. On the bar top was a folded newspaper with the headline half-obscured: 'Whereabouts Still Unknown,' it read. From the street a horn sounded. The priest stepped out of the bar and approached a jeep with three Guardia Civil officers inside, greeted them, and got in the back seat. The morning was foggy. On the motorway from the city to the mountains, all that could be seen were the white lines of the road. A man with a moustache was at the wheel. The lines curved and the car followed their turns. Then the jeep went up and down a few hills, finally reaching an open-air restaurant. The men got out. The collarless priest led the expedition to a gravel road that ended at a rocky slope. The priest grabbed a tree branch to pull himself up. When he reached the top, he took a quartz pendulum out of his pocket and showed it to his companions. They walked on until they reached an empty field. The priest spread a map on a tree stump and took the pendulum out again. The quartz spun over a river. The four men followed the riverbed to its source, cut several branches, shouted my grandfather's name, but found nothing.

My father visited an old woman who worked with the collarless priest and read cards in a village near San Sebastián. The first time he came in, she was waiting for him with half a deck laid out on the table mat. When she saw him, she peered over her glasses: 'I don't know why I'm not seeing anything,' she said, and she tapped three times on the wedge of remaining cards on the table. A fool, a magician, an empress and a hierophant were resting face up on the felt. The woman held out her arm and said: 'Take my hand and maybe together we'll see.' The two of them closed their eyes and were silent for a while, but all they saw was the inside of their eye sockets.

There was a knock at the door. The old woman got up from her chair and let in the priest, who was back from the mountain. The priest was out of breath and the soles of his boots were muddy; he spread the map on the floor and said: 'The pendulum says he's on the riverbank, but in the river there are nothing but toads.' Then he took off his boots, combed his grey hair with his fingers and picked up a newspaper. My father and the old woman went back to studying the figures on the felt. Meanwhile, the priest pulled a stool up to the table and sat down to solve the crossword puzzle.

*

On the 16th, 17th and 18th of June 1977, a number of calls were made to the local paper. Most were from people with jobs affording them ample leisure time: concierges, night watchmen, salesgirls at fabric shops on side streets. All complained about the same thing: 'I've been trying to do the crossword puzzle, but I don't get it.'

The 16 June crossword puzzle, once solved, read across as follows: 'Dear pris of this. See key to letters. Third letter first words.' The one on the 17th read: 'Lame of leg, write family secret message. Third letter each line to the break. Ladylike mushrooms.' And the one on the 18th, the last day of the period given by the kidnappers for the delivery of the ransom: 'Waiting for letter. Key. The third letter each line. Luck. Tiny hope.'

Along with the crosswords, the rest of the puzzles had hidden messages too. The word games of 16 and 17 June are the most obvious:

QUESTION:

Will there be a reward?

PUZZLE:

EYE (I)

SHKSPR (Will)

AGAIN (Re)

−DROBE (Ward)

+SONG (Hymn)

ANSWER:

I will reward him

QUESTION:

Will you turn in your tormentor?

PUZZLE:

EYE-F (If)

EYE (I)

ULLMAN (Liv)

MA-S (Mum's)

EL OR LA (The)

-SMITH (Word)

ANSWER:

If I live, mum's the word.

To attract my grandfather's attention, it was decided to swap out the Spot the Difference comics. These drawings were usually by the Belgian cartoonist Jean Laplace, but on the 16th, 17th and 18th of June 1977, some anonymous sketches appeared, depicting two buildings owned by my family as well as the juvenile detention centre in Amurrio, of which my grandfather was trustee. Across from the three buildings, a man with a big round nose asks a dog for help in solving a crossword puzzle. In the 16 June cartoon, the man and the dog are sitting. On the 17th and 18th, they're standing.

'We don't know anything about the puzzles. We've never used them as a way to contact our father,' said the siblings to the press. 'We're taking all the usual steps through our lawyers,' commented my father's oldest brother. According to some news reports, my grandfather gave no indication in his letters of having received coded messages. Others, meanwhile, were less certain: according to them, the key to the communion box was part of some conversation.

*

The month of June was passing, and with it the period for delivering the ransom. The older siblings spoke to the lawyers and the younger ones whiled away the hours in the chapel at home. They hadn't been able to raise much money. Though the kidnappers demanded a ransom from the whole family, only the siblings were willing to shoulder the responsibility. The banks weren't helpful, either. Bankers from the two institutions consulted said that it wasn't possible to lend money to a kidnapping victim and that fifty million was the most they could offer. To raise that amount, the siblings had to sign a policy in which they pledged to be jointly responsible for the loan. They tried to mortgage their father's properties in exchange for more, but the response was always the same: 'We can't lend money to a man who's been kidnapped.'

Night fell. The youngest brother ranted brokenly and shouted 'sons of bitches'. The circles under his eyes were darker than ever. The other siblings slept fitfully, clutching each other in pairs, regardless of sex. No one went into the back bedroom. Only Marcelina, the maid, approached the door with a vacuum cleaner, but she couldn't bring herself to turn the knob. In the living room, the oldest brother composed a letter to send to the press:

> In my own name and that of my siblings, I wish to convey our grave concern for the fate of our dear father, kidnapped this past 20 May.

Additionally, we would like to make very clear that the requests for a billion pesetas in exchange for his life are completely out of our reach. Faced with the impossibility of satisfying these demands, we have tried and will continue to try by all means possible to reach an agreement that will lead to his release.

Regarding the announcement that our father will be executed if the required sum is not delivered, and that the very great responsibility for his life lies in our hands, we would like to state that those who hold our father captive are the sole arbiters of his fate.

*

The collarless priest was almost sure that my grandfather was being held somewhere on Mount Gorbea. The morning of 18 June, 1977, the last day of the period for delivering the ransom, the priest returned to the mountains with a convoy of thirty Guardia Civil officers. When he reached Alto de Barazar, he took out a map of the search area and spun his quartz. When the pendulum stopped, he got out a larger-scale map and repeated the operation to narrow the hunt. Behind him were fifteen jeeps parked in rows, and some Guardia Civil officers clearing people from a restaurant. The terrace was deserted, occupied only by plastic tables with umbrella poles sticking up from the middle. It began to rain hard, but the expedition didn't come to a halt. The men put on their cloaks and scattered to cover the areas marked on the map.

A Guardia Civil officer with his feet sinking into the mud spotted a light deep in a beech grove. The glow came from a hut built from scrap: rough half-painted planks, rusty nails and broken tiles. From the chimney — a length of sawed-off pipe — a narrow column of grey smoke rose. The shack was home to El Escobero, an old maker of straw brooms, who now occupied himself twisting rope for horse hobbles. The officer knocked. He heard uncertain footsteps and thumps on the floor, then keys turning and clattering against the doorframe. The door opened and there stood a man with a long beard the same shape and colour as the column of smoke rising from the chimney. He was naked from the waist up and his nipples were tiny. People called him Robinson the Broom Man. 'Haven't seen or heard anything,' he said. 'There was just one car all weekend, Madrid licence plate, lost and driving in circles.'

The Guardia Civil officer took down El Escobero's statement. Then he showed him a piece of plastic and a wet blanket. When he saw the objects, the shack's inhabitant shrugged and slowly closed the door.

*

At 5 p.m. on 18 June, 1977, an announcer on Radio Popular interrupted the broadcast to report that Javier Ybarra had been killed and that his body was somewhere off a forest trail in the vicinity of Alto de Barazar, in the same area on the map indicated by the priest's quartz pendulum. The Guardia Civil was asking for more troops to comb the stands of beech and pine, but the rain was so heavy that it was hard to see anything. A few hours later, several anonymous calls to the same radio station claimed that my grandfather was still alive and that the afternoon report was false. At one in the morning, it was still unconfirmed.

The search operation went on for three and a half days longer, though no one knew whether the man they were looking for was alive or dead. On 22 June, 1977, at 4 p.m., more loose sheets of paper turned up in a San Sebastián mailbox. They were signed by the kidnappers and they said that my grandfather's body was in the place described in their first message, and that if the police hadn't found the body, it was because they didn't know how to look. The text made constant reference to two other documents that were nowhere to be found. At 6 p.m., two balled-up sheets of notebook paper were discovered in a waste-paper basket at the central post office. Upon smoothing them out, the postman read the following message:

> Javier Ybarra was killed a few hours after 3 p.m. on 18 June, 1977.
>
> Cenauri-Vitoria highway. From Alto de Barazar, take the path that leads from the right side of the bar-restaurant to a kind of workshop with a corrugated roof, next to a private lodge. A few metres before the lodge is a forest trail. Follow this trail for about three hundred metres, and among some pines to the left is the body. It is covered by a dark grey plastic sheet and some branches.

1. LODGE: white walls with two orange windows

    can be seen from Number 2

    there's a door in the middle

    looks new

    not to be confused with the private lodge

2. AREA WITH NO PINE TREES: surrounded by pine trees

    towards the centre is a tree with big branches

    horses grazing

3. AREA WITH PINE TREES: deep shade, the sun hardly shines

    trees grow very close together

    small hill

    from the path you can't SEE THE BODY

    it is about 30 (thirty) metres from the trail (RIP) [written in pen]

    RIP here he lies in the PEACE OF THE LORD (according to him) and thanks to his family

At the end of the text there is a map with the letters *RIP-J.I.* marking the location of the body.

*

The search was begun again with more men. At a quarter to seven on the evening of Wednesday, 22 June, my grandfather's body was found under a heavy sheet of grey plastic. When the body was uncovered, a small quantity of blood ran out.

The body, with a gunshot wound to the head, was inside a plastic bag hooked on a nail, the victim blindfolded, his arms tied behind his back. During his captivity he had lost 22 kilos and his clothes smelled of urine and excrement. Upon performing the autopsy, Doctor Toledo, medical examiner at Basurto Hospital, determined that his intestinal walls were atrophied, evidence that [...] he had been given almost nothing to eat during his confinement. His body was also covered in sores, a clear sign that he had spent the duration in a prone position or inside a sack that prevented movement.[1]

The description of the trajectory of the bullet that killed him is as follows:

> [...] entrance via the left posterior occipitotemporal lobe and exit via the right frontal region at an oblique angle, bottom to top and left to right. Death was instantaneous [...]
>
> *ABC*, 23 June, 1977

---

1. *Los mitos del nacionalismo vasco,* José Díaz Herrera, Planeta, 2005.

VI

ABC, 26 June, 1977. I zoom out on the page to get a full view of the photograph and the headlines. To the left, a bearded reporter in a blazer holds a notepad. To the right, my father and two of his brothers, all dressed in black, stand in a semicircle around him. All of them, including the reporter, have their heads bowed. My uncles are silent and my father is speaking. 'From our special correspondents in Bilbao,' says the newspaper.

When we were informed that our father's body had been found, I decided to get the car and drive up to Alto de Barazar. I was advised not to go, as the motorway could be mined. But we set out anyway in Rogelio the mechanic's SEAT 850, very slowly. We stopped, and on the motorway I flagged down a 1430, which took us the rest of the way at top speed. I didn't know the driver. His name was Zabala.

We finally reached Alto de Barazar. To get from the spot where the news photographers were to the place where the body was took us a while. It was hard going and there were several forks in the path, and we chose one or another at random. Zabala came along with me, like a good friend, a Good Samaritan. We got to where the police jeeps and buses were.

His body was in a deep gully, densely overgrown. You had to work your way in to see it. He was on the ground, his body at an angle on the slope, face up, with a four-day-old white beard. There was an expression of great serenity and dignity on his face. He was covered with a heavy, grey plastic sheet. Next to him was his raincoat, rolled up, and, within reach of his right hand, the missal that he used every day, a prayer book, the rosary and his glasses. Also an inhaler. Though he didn't have asthma, he did have some trouble with his breathing and he sometimes suffered from spells of fatigue.

My father used to wear out his shoes walking. He loved to go tramping in the mountains. Now he's lost his life on a peak. He used to hike in his canvas shoes, even though he had been wounded in the war and had a limp.

*

After reading my father's statement in the paper, I googled 'Javier Ybarra killed'. Among the photographs that turned up was one showing several men lifting my grandfather's body into a hearse. The body is covered by a white blanket and everyone except for the driver is dressed in civilian clothes. I searched for my father among them, but couldn't find him. I know from the newspaper that my father had followed my grandfather to the hospital in Zabala's car. Behind them came a bus and thirteen jeeps full of Guardia Civil officers and loggers who had taken part in the search. When word spread that his body had been found, one of the local radio stations interrupted its programming to play hymns.

The procession filed down the mountain and made its way in a long line to Basurto Hospital, where my father's oldest brother and some twenty reporters were waiting. It was eighteen minutes before my grandfather's body emerged from the back of the hearse. At 12.25 a.m. the body was lifted out, covered in a blanket and the reporters rushed to take photographs, but they couldn't because my father blocked the way. Before the start of the autopsy, the medical examiner handed my father's oldest brother a gold ring and chain. At approximately a quarter to one in the morning, the siblings left the mortuary to head home. The autopsy had begun.

During the autopsy it was discovered that my grandfather had traces of grass in his stomach and that it had been at least three days since he'd defecated, even though excrement was discovered in the hideout that the police found some time later. It was in a half-collapsed farmhouse, with boards nailed over the windows and bricked-up doors. They also found the remains of two fires and a piece of the sweater that my grandfather was wearing the day that he was kidnapped. This section of Alto de Barazar wasn't searched when the hunt for the body was underway.

VII

The funeral took place on 23 June, 1977, at 6 p.m. in the parish of San Ignacio, Getxo. The Mass for the dead was celebrated by ten priests. Most of those in attendance, local people, had received at least one sacrament in the church. There were many worshippers, so many that the church had to hang a pair of speakers from the eaves so the ceremony could be heard in the grounds.

My father and his siblings kneeled in the front row with their hands over their faces. A few reporters crouched before them and photographed them. There was a ringing of bells and the photographers covered their lenses and went up into the balcony. Mass was about to begin. The ten priests in purple cassocks filed in from the sacristy. They approached the altar from one side and stood in two semicircles around the Christ of splintered wood that presided over the church. Just in front, slightly below, was the raised bier.

It was a long service, the sermons brief. When it ended, my father and his brothers went up to the altar to carry the coffin to the hearse. There were so many people in the church that it wasn't easy to get through. The brothers advanced slowly, rocking the box from side to side to make way. No one spoke. The quiet was interrupted only by a man shouting 'Death to the killers! Death to the killers!' but he was quickly silenced.

The cortège set off towards the Derio cemetery. Every one hundred metres, Guardia Civil officers saluted the procession from the kerb. Some townspeople stood by the side of the road, too, to pay their respects.

VIII

There's almost no resemblance. The ear looks bigger, the nose sharper. The photograph of my grandfather's body that I view in Google Images has little in common with the portrait of him in the living room. I look at the two pictures, searching for differences: longer hair, longer beard, thinner.

My grandfather Javier was mayor of Bilbao from 1963 to 1969, as well as president of the Provincial Council of Vizcaya from 1947 to 1950, of the newspaper *El Correo Español-El Pueblo Vasco,* and of the Bilbao juvenile court. He was also a consultant to various companies, a member of the Royal Academy of History and author of ten books on the province of Vizcaya. He had a slight limp, having been wounded in the right knee during the Battle of the Ebro in the Civil War.

ETA had him in its sights because it considered him the epitome of the Neguri intellectual and because he belonged to one of the families that had traditionally occupied top posts in the province. The group saw him as a symbol of central government power. Three days before his death, on 15 June, 1977, the first elections of the new democracy were held. My grandfather's killing was condemned in the media and rejected by all political groups, but no one took to the streets to protest. 'If he was killed, it must be because he did something wrong.'

*

The name of the district of Neguri comes from the combination of two Basque words: *negua* and *hiri*, or winter and city, which are a vestige of the publicity slogan with which the area was promoted: 'For winter too.' Until the arrival of the railroad in 1903, it had been mostly a neighbourhood of summer people, but with the construction of the train lines, new residents began to move in and built palaces on the beach, a tennis club, a clay pigeon shooting gallery and a golf course. The area's period of greatest splendour lasted until the thirties: the neighbourhood families got rich on the proceeds of blast furnaces, banks, mines and shipping companies. When my grandfather died, at the end of the seventies, business was in decline. The factories had become obsolete, though a few people still lived off their income. Some heirs struggled to resurrect family empires, while others spent their days wandering the tennis club, the yacht club and the golf club. In 1983, the year that I was born, a flood finally swamped Vizcaya's ailing industry. The Estuary of Bilbao, once a global symbol of progress, was now a muddy wasteland full of crumbling blast furnaces.

*

At the beginning of the eighties, an air of defeat settled over the neighbourhood. The fall of the Franco regime had coincided with the oil crisis and with ETA's first assassinations in the province. Many residents imagined that they were going to inherit great fortunes, but it was not to be. Some felt nostalgia for the glorious past. Others checked out. Heroin, hashish, sex and cocaine were consumed in a van that circled the streets near the train station, driven by a blonde woman. The seeming calm of the comfortable houses and gardens with clipped hedges was interrupted every so often by threats, disappearances and deaths. The first ETA attack in the neighbourhood came on 26 November, 1973. A hooded man sprayed gasoline on the ground floor of the yacht club and started a fire that burned down the building. In the following months it was rebuilt in concrete and steel, but on 19 May, 2008, the explosion of a van left the back side of the club in ruins once again. During the roughest years at the beginning of the eighties – the so-called *años de plomo*, or Years of Lead – the neighbours pretended that nothing was happening: they played tennis, had cocktails, went out sailing and visited the open-air restaurants of Berango. The tension was under wraps. A car in flames, a dead body, and a few hours later everything seemed to return to normal.

If a death threat was received, it was only discussed in private, never with casual acquaintances. Few felt they had the right to voice their discontent. Between 1973 and 2008, ETA planted a number of bombs in the neighbourhood and kidnapped a few residents. Many families sold their homes at a loss and left the Basque Country. We moved in '95. The day my mother told me we had to go, I had just come back from a school trip to the pine groves of Azkorri. It was almost the end of the year, my sixth in primary school. My mother was boiling water in a pot. 'We have to move to Madrid,' she said. I didn't cry in front of her. But I did later, when I told my two best friends that weekend.

I knew there were people who wanted to kill my father. Sometimes I watched him transcribing an interview or reading a book and I tried to understand why. Most of the time I wasn't afraid, except when there was some clear danger. Otherwise, I lived at a remove from the conflict. The stories about 'La ETA' and my grandfather's killing were mixed with others that my father told me about Pompeii, Degas's ballerinas, Darío's 'The princess is sad' poem, and Max Ernst's bird men.

TWO

TWO

I

The surgeon who filed the bridge of my mother's nose didn't do a good job of shaping the wings, so the end of her nose looked like a half-inflated ball. I imagine the big bulbs of the surgery lamp illuminating the nurses' covered heads and my adolescent mother anesthetised on the hospital bed dreaming about wheat fields in summer.

After the procedure, she was supposed to tend the scars for a few months and go back to the doctor so that he could redo her nose. She never went. She got used to the imperfect wings. The operation had been my grandmother's idea. The beak of her own nose was even sharper and she didn't like to be reminded of it on someone else's face. I inherited it too, though mine is only a small bump that my mother liked to stroke.

My mother was the kind of person who felt little attachment to places, objects and her own body. When she died, the only belongings that we had to go through were her clothes and shoes. Nothing else was exclusively hers. At home, she spent most of her time in the office, but even so, nothing in the room belonged just to her. She wasn't bothered by birthdays, or new places. When we moved to Madrid, it took her scarcely any time to get used to the city. When she was admitted to the hospital, she immediately belonged to the hospital.

*

My mother's death brought back my grandfather's death. Before it, the killing was just a pair of handcuffs in a glass case next to the bronze llamas that my parents had brought back from Peru. The tedium of illness recalled the tedium of the wait during the kidnapping. My father began to talk about blood-stained rosaries. It would be months yet before I could understand his pain.

II

The afternoon of 4 April, 2011, my mother called me and said: 'Gabriela, I have cancer, but it's really nothing.' A few hours later she boarded a plane and sat on her tumour all the way to New York. As she and my father were driving to the airport, I went to Bryant Park to sit in front of the hotel where they had stayed three weeks earlier, when they came to the city to visit me.

The afternoon of the call, I explained to my boss that I needed to go out and get some air. Bryant Park was just two blocks from the office. I crossed Times Square, and when I got to the park I sat on a green café chair at the edge of the lawn. Two minutes later I dialled Manhattan Oncology Center. 'I need an appointment for my mother,' I said to the woman who answered the phone. 'I can't help you, everyone is gone, I'm the cleaning lady,' she said. 'So what do I do until tomorrow?' I asked. 'There's nothing you can do,' she said.

My mother wanted an appointment with Doctor Marsden, a surgeon she had heard good things about; she had told me so on the phone. I googled Doctor Marsden and decided that he was good looking. My mother thought so too. Soon afterwards, a friend of a friend of my mother's called. It was someone I didn't know, but he had the email of the wife of one of the doctor's patients. From my café chair in Bryant Park I wrote an email to the woman asking her for help. The woman replied a few minutes later, saying I had to write to Luke; that Luke would help us. I wrote to Luke, Luke got back to me quickly and said that Doctor Marsden would see us in a week. When my mother landed I told her that I'd made her an appointment with the surgeon. 'How did you do it?' she asked.

*

Before my mother's diagnosis, I didn't pay much attention to death. And I didn't think much about it over the course of the treatment, either. During the hour and a half that I sat in Bryant Park, I contemplated the fact that the first time I'd heard about her tumour had been in this same place three weeks before. When she'd sat down on one of the café chairs in the park, my mother remarked that she had to rest her weight on one buttock because if she didn't then her bum hurt a lot. She said the word *bum* in a low voice, and then more loudly she said: 'I've got a strange pimple.' In those days I still believed that premature death belonged to the realm of fiction.

I don't think that my mother thought of death as fiction. In the years leading up to her diagnosis, she had borne close witness to her parents' illnesses; and before that, when my father received kidnapping threats that never materialised, she remembered her father-in-law and was afraid that something of the same kind could happen to us.

The afternoon that I spent sitting in Bryant Park, I remembered my mother's parents. Both of them died of cancer. When each was ill, my mother spent a lot of time with them: visiting one doctor or another, playing cards . . . Her siblings helped when they could. Two of them didn't live in Madrid, and the third swapped shifts with her when he wasn't at work. My family always felt that not enough was done to save my grandfather; they thought that the doctors had given him up for lost too soon, and that in the United States it wouldn't have happened. Years later, around 2004, it was discovered that my grandmother had a brain tumour. Her children decided that she would be operated on in Los Angeles. The operation went well, and a few weeks later she was back in Madrid, where she continued her treatment. My mother and her siblings found a doctor who had a degree from Oxford and whose office was full of awards and diplomas. This gave them confidence. When my mother got sick, the United States was the only option she considered.

*

I still don't know much about the day when her tumour was discovered. The only information I have is what my father wrote in his diary:

Start of Ernestina's illness. Husband's notes.

Madrid. Wednesday, 23 March, 2011. Appointment with Doctor Herreros after surgical procedure/biopsy.
The tumour is very localised, in a pre-existing fissure in the anus. It is a hairy polyp with some cancerous cells at the base. It

is small, flat, adhering to the sphincter, and a scar was left when it was removed. Will have to excise the scar to see whether there are traces of the tumour underneath. Operating seems to be the best option, but it must be done carefully so as not to damage the sphincter. If it's skilfully done it shouldn't be necessary to implant an artificial anus. The lesion is very localised, external and was detected early. Before operating, a three-week wait is required for the wound to heal. Meanwhile, the following tests can be performed: endoscopic ultrasound, X-ray, MRI, probe and TAC.

These notes were taken by her husband, in longhand, during the appointment.

*

It all happened very quickly. From the time of her diagnosis until she died was just six months. I can't remember my parents' arrival in New York and I'm not sure whether it was on this trip or another one that they spent a few nights in a room where the refrigerator vibrated so much that they couldn't sleep. My mother's first few days in Manhattan were spent shopping. We bought clothes at the Ann Taylor on Madison Avenue that were instantly too big for her because she lost so much weight during the treatment. Among other things, she bought the jeans that I have on now. My mother had always been very thin, but in the months that followed my grandfather's death she had aged all of a sudden, her metabolism changed, her face and hips widened and her belly grew round. Over the past few years she had gained even more weight and she went to the gym often, though she didn't like it and wasn't good at it. After she died, I gained a lot of weight too. From the back I look like her. I've signed up for Pilates classes. I wore her tracksuit for several months until last time I went on holiday I left it in the washing machine and it got mouldy.

III

The day that they performed the first colonoscopy, I was sitting behind a blue curtain in the same room. I could see the shoes of the oncologist moving on the tiles from one side of the hospital bed to the other, and the amplified colon on a screen. I got my phone out of my pocket and took a photo of the monitor. In the centre of the image there was a black hole surrounded by hazy white rings that reminded me of a weather map.

The oncologist drew back the curtain and began to talk. At first my mother watched him, but then she turned to me, letting me know that she didn't understand his jargon. The doctor said that he hadn't seen anything, that when the tissue sample was taken the entire tumour seemed to have been removed. 'I don't think it will be necessary to operate,' he said. I translated this for my mother and she nodded. The doctor began to talk again. He repeated the word *ulcerated*. We didn't know whether *ulcerated* was serious or not, but it sounded bad. When he said *ulcerated* he didn't appear concerned. Then he said *chemotherapy* and *radiation therapy*. My mother and I nodded. *Next week.* We nodded again.

We met Doctor Marsden an hour later. His office was on the same floor as the oncologist's, the third floor of the Manhattan

Oncology Center building on 65th St. After we left the first doctor's office, my mother and I met my father in the waiting room. We said: 'It looks like it won't be necessary to operate.' My father said something about scraping out the remains of the tumour. My mother pretended not to hear him. She sat down next to him and took out her phone to look at the picture of the surgeon that she had downloaded from the Internet. From my seat I studied the other patients. It struck me that no one looked sick; everyone who walked in and out of the elevators had hair and strode confidently. My father didn't understand how the tumour could disappear; to me, on the other hand, it seemed perfectly natural.

Doctor Marsden's assistant came out to get us after a while. Once we were in the office, I recognised the mane of white hair and the wire-framed glasses from the photograph on the phone. In front of the surgeon was a desk scattered with images of my mother's colon. Doctor Marsden picked up one of them and said again that he didn't see anything to remove. Nevertheless, both he and the oncologist believed that it was important to pursue treatment in case any cancerous cell was still lurking and began to multiply again. Eight weeks of radiation therapy and chemotherapy and then back to Madrid. That was the original plan. 'You'll live to see your grandchildren,' Doctor Marsden said to my mother before we left.

Sometimes I wonder why my mother didn't go back to Madrid after this trip. I think partly it was because she wanted to be with me. She chose me to be the one to take care of her. I quit my job and she liked that. On the other hand, I think that she also needed a change of scene. She didn't want to see the same doctors who had treated my grandparents or to visit the same hospitals. In New York everything was new, from the streets to the language. The stress in *tumour* fell on the *tu* rather than the *mour; cahn-ther* became *can-cer.*

IV

Lately I feel the need to go back to the hospital. I believe dates are important; anniversaries must be marked. My mother died on a Tuesday, and I remember her every Tuesday. My mother died on the 6th, and I think of her every 6th. Maybe this is why a few days ago I began to consciously repeat some of the things that happened to me a year ago, when she was sick. This week, for example, I called the guy I slept with the day after she had her first colonoscopy at the hospital. 'It's been a while since we saw each other,' I said when he answered the phone. 'We could get a drink,' he replied. And this Monday he asked me out to dinner at a restaurant a few blocks from my house, not his kind of place and beyond his means. When I got there, he was waiting for me at the entrance. His hair had grown an inch and a half and he was wearing Cuban-heeled boots that suited him. He spotted me right away, kissed me on the cheek and said several times that I looked nice. Then he recognised the tight blue trousers from our last date and reached out to touch my arse, but didn't dare. We went into the restaurant and were seated at a table near the window. The food was expensive; to judge by his intake of breath, quite a bit more expensive than he had anticipated. We ordered the two cheapest entrées on the menu and a bottle of California wine. Dinner was painful. The wine failed to flow and the conversation stalled. I talked a lot about my mother, about my internship that year, and he kept laughing. 'This is all really funny,' he said, when I wasn't trying to be humorous. I decided to stop talking. He began to wag his head back and forth as he chewed; he fidgeted in his chair and glanced around the restaurant as I ate heartily in silence. He didn't finish his meal. He paid the bill and we took a taxi to his apartment in Bed-Stuy. During the ride we kissed and I stroked his thigh through his trousers. As I did, I wondered whether he would be wearing the same ugly brown underwear he'd had on the last time. His apartment was disgusting. There were pizza boxes stacked in the kitchen and a thick layer of grime in the bathroom. He undressed me by the door and led me to bed. The sex was good. We did it again the next morning, but soon after we finished I told him I had to go. I sat on the damp sheets and searched for my underwear on the floor. As I was getting dressed I thought about my mother. About the same day the year before when, after I'd slept with the same guy, I'd gone home to shower and I'd met her for lunch at a Mexican restaurant. Now he was kissing my neck, trying to keep me from leaving. He took a bandana out of a drawer and put it on his head. 'Women like how I look in this,' he said. I felt ridiculous for having slept with someone like him. I got a taxi and went home. I showered and ordered fajitas at a Mexican restaurant.

*

Friday, 10 August, 2012

Today I've come back to the first hospital waiting room I visited with my parents. The treatment began here more than a year ago now, on the third floor of the Manhattan Oncology Center building on 65th St. From my seat I can see a coffee machine and a television with the volume off. No one is reading, but at the back of the room two Russian women are knitting.

The room is big. You might call it studiedly pleasant, with plants, flowers, a rug and well-upholstered sofas. There are many people; maybe sixty. Of them all, the one who catches my eye is a black-haired man in a purple argyle sweater.

The man is older, but there's no grey in his hair. Every so often he bows over the table and rests his forehead on his fist. It looks as if he's praying. The man in the sweater rubs his nose. He does it very slowly. He gets up; he has a limp. It's hard to say whether it's a physical impediment or whether he's paralysed by sorrow. The man takes a coffee cup and pushes the button on the machine with a slow, heavy finger.

At the back of the room, on the long sofas, there's a family in which everyone is wearing turbans. To my right is a man with a striped tie, on the phone with his insurance company. He wants to know whether they will cover some pills. When he reads the prescription he mentions my mother's oncologist. I had forgotten his name, and now I feel as if I don't remember anything.

An older woman is taking a bite of a slice of pizza that her daughter has brought her. She chews with pleasure, nudging in the bits that escape the sides of her mouth. Her daughter is bored and doesn't talk much. Now she's picking the hairs off her mother's jacket. The woman looks at me as if she knows that I'm writing about her and she turns her head away to let me keep observing her.

To my left, a big-kneed woman asks me whether I mind if she eats a sandwich, though what she really wants is to talk. She tells me that she used to be a nurse and that unfortunately she's very familiar with the protocols. 'At this hospital, it's all about numbers, data and facts. If you still have hair and you can walk, you'll be starting your treatment on the third floor.' The man who was on the phone with his insurance company breaks in. 'If you're here, you have cancer,' he says. I fall silent, and now it's just the two of them talking, exchanging their views on holiday-morning staff shortages.

V

Doctor Spring warned us that radiation therapy would bring on menopause. Then she told us that it would also cause shrinking of the vagina, and she picked up a green case from her desk. She opened it and took out several little plastic-wrapped tubes in different sizes. The thinnest was as big around as a permanent marker and the thickest a small zucchini. As the doctor was talking, my mother looked at the zip of her trousers.

'It's important to insert this tube into your vagina for a few hours a day when the treatment is over. Little by little, you'll notice the walls stretching. I also recommend that you maintain an active sex life,' and she reached over to hand us a pamphlet titled 'Sexual Health'.

Then the doctor went on explaining the effects of the treatment.

'You won't lose your hair, but you'll have trouble controlling the urge to go to the bathroom; it might be a good idea to wear a nappy. Put it on before you go out, in case you have to go halfway down the street. Either way, I recommend that you buy disposable panties.'

My mother raised her head to stare at the doctor.

'From Monday to Friday you'll have radiation therapy. The preparation and treatment will take about three hours altogether, so if you arrive at nine you won't be out of the hospital until twelve. On Mondays at three you'll have to go to the 65th St building for tests and to have the chemo pump changed. On Tuesdays at four thirty you'll have an appointment with the oncologist, and on Wednesdays at two thirty with me, to see how the radiation is going. Otherwise, you can lead a completely normal life. If you work, I encourage you not to stop, and of course you can be out and about, take day trips, go to the supermarket . . . though you might tire more easily than usual and you'll need extra sleep.'

My mother eyed the little plastic tube on the edge of the table.

'Be careful with food. Your stomach will be sensitive from the treatment. You should eat mostly protein, and limit vegetables as much as possible. I've made you an appointment for tomorrow with a nutritionist who will explain in more detail how you should eat. I also recommend not wearing trousers and buying some skirts; trousers will chafe the radiated area, which will be a little bit irritated.' At this point the doctor took a piece of paper out of the drawer and showed it to us. 'Look, this is the spot. The remains of the tumour that we want to radiate are at the end of the colon, so it's the pelvic area that will be most affected. It will feel like a sunburn, but don't worry, we'll give you an ointment for pain relief.'

At this point the little tube fell off the table, rolling against the doctor's foot. The doctor bent down, picked it up and threw it in a rubbish bin as she kept talking.

'Tomorrow you have an appointment at the 65th St building for placement of the Mediport, the catheter through which the chemo will be administered. It doesn't take long to get used to it and it isn't especially painful. In fact, in surveys of our patients, 85 per cent say that they're comfortable with their Mediports.'

My mother was looking at the rubbish bin now.

The doctor swivelled in her chair and put the paper back in the drawer. When she turned to us again, she saw my mother's face and she said, 'I know it's a lot, but don't worry. As far as circumstances allow, you'll be able to continue to live a more or less normal life. If you have any questions, don't hesitate to call me; otherwise, I'll see you next Wednesday at the same time,' and she shook our hands.

'Oh, and remember to always wear a hat and a high-factor sun cream if you go out,' the doctor said, coming to the door.

My mother and I left the hospital. In my hand were the prescriptions: disposable panties, nappies, ointment for the pelvic region, anti-diarrhoea pills and sun cream. Next to me, my mother was carrying the green case of little tubes and looking through the pamphlet.

*

The Midtown Barnes & Noble we stopped at was across the street. I had long hair and the sales assistant stared at it. My mother and I were on our way back from her first radiation therapy appointment and she had just got her period. She was bleeding a lot. This was the last time she would menstruate. As we rode up to the music section in the store I imagined my mother going into a big round tube, her ovaries full, and coming out sterile. I knew they put music on during the treatment.

'I listened to The Beatles,' she said. 'They say I can bring in anything I want,' and we went to a Barnes & Noble to buy one of ABBA's greatest hits albums.

The next morning, as I watched her go into the changing room at the hospital, I couldn't help imagining her singing along inside the machine to the Swedish group's choruses.

*

Doctor Spring, who had an undergraduate degree from Yale and multiple master's degrees, was also very attractive. She wore heels and eyeliner, and she knew how to put on lip liner without looking vulgar. 'Did you go to the bathroom all right?' she asked my mother at the second appointment. 'How many times a day? Have you had any soreness in the pelvic or rectal area? Lie down here so I can see how the skin looks in the radiated area. Is the ointment working? How has your last period been? Don't worry if you're bleeding a lot, it's normal.' The doctor put on latex gloves and drew a curtain so that I couldn't see her examining my mother. 'Your skin looks wonderful, just a little bit red,' she said as she felt under my mother's skirt. 'Is your food going down well?' 'The other day I had fish and I threw up,' answered my mother, 'but otherwise, everything's fine.' 'Good,' said the doctor, 'you're a fantastic patient.' Then she took two steps towards the curtain, the toes of her purple pumps pointing at me before she pulled it aside. 'Your mother is progressing nicely,' she said when the curtain was drawn back. 'It's important to walk a lot, and walk quickly,' and she swivelled her hips gracefully to indicate speed. 'Next week my assistant will see you because I'll be on vacation in Italy.' 'Where in Italy?' asked my mother. 'Sardinia,' said the doctor. 'My husband's treat, we've been married for ten years and we were there on our honeymoon.'

Doctor Spring, slender and elegant, took off the used gloves and threw them in the bin. My mother adjusted her skirt, her hat, the hip pack with the chemotherapy pump, looked at the doctor and felt like a piece of trash.

VI

Most of the time I don't think about it. Only when I brush my hair in front of the mirror and I see the single grey hair that sticks up from the crown of my head. Other times, when I'm lying in bed, I concentrate on my body inflating and deflating and I become aware of being mortal. A few weeks ago I decided to change my diet. Now I eat organic fruits and vegetables and fish. My skin is smoother than it's ever been. In the mirror, parts of my face look babyish, but I'm not a child. I spend whole days watching YouTube videos of girls doing their hair and trying on lipstick. I take notes. I chart the users. I write down quotes and ideas for the product development department of a cosmetics multinational. With each market study I develop a new obsession. I switched deodorants because the one I was using had aluminium in it and could cause cancer, I spent a week analysing the length of my eyelashes, and I threw away several bottles of shampoo that contained silicone. I can spend an entire afternoon contemplating what my beauty routine says about me, even though some nights I don't brush my teeth before bed.

I started to do market studies of cosmetic products when my mother got sick. It was my friend Sonia's idea. Since I couldn't go into an office and I had a lot of dead time in the hospital, she thought it might be a good way to make some money. My first assignment was a study of hairsprays on the German market. As my mother was receiving radiation therapy, I watched YouTube videos of men and women doing their hair. I wrote down the names of the products they preferred, whether they used conditioners or curling tongs, what distance they held the dryer from their heads. I classified the kinds of brushes, the users' comments on the feel of a particular hairspray in their hair, and their impressions of the packaging and advertising.

It had been years since I'd read or heard German. It's a language closely linked to my childhood, and the sound of it makes me feel safe because it reminds me of my grandfather Ricardo, nursery school and the words to the Nena song '99 Luftballons'. In German everything seemed more appealing to me than in Spanish. When I was eighteen I stopped speaking it. I went away to school, and that was the end of the summers spent perfecting my accent on horse farms outside of Cologne and Hanover. My grandfather, of German descent and worried about preserving his heritage, had died a few years before. While my mother received radiation therapy, I sought refuge on YouTube among girls who talked to me about hairspray in musical words and tones that I hadn't heard for ten years.

*

Thursday, 23 August, 2012

Today I've come back to visit the radiation waiting room in the hospital's main building on East End Avenue. At the 80th St entrance it smells like disinfectant and it's cold. Depending on which door you come in, it's hard to get your bearings. Most of the signs are for letters: Q & Z to the left, B & J to the right. I was looking for R. I got into an elevator, followed by a man holding an oxygen tank, two nurses, and a woman carrying a little girl dressed as a princess. When we got to the second floor, there was a jolt, the same jolt the elevator used to give when my mother was here for treatment. The little girl in the costume tried to jump out of her mother's arms and the man with the tank said something to one of the nurses.

Now I'm sitting in an ugly but very comfortable grey chair, in the radiation waiting room. I've just stretched out my legs. Next to me is a man in a wheelchair wearing blue pyjamas. 'I'm from Connecticut,' he tells me. He doesn't seem to care that I'm taking notes. 'They want to operate on me but they don't know if I'll survive the operation.' I stop writing and look at him: 'I'm sorry.' 'I'm eighty years old,' he says. I'm prepared to continue the conversation, but a nurse comes over, says the man's last name and pushes his wheelchair down the hallway. I pick up a magazine but I can't concentrate. I try a glossier one. I feel the same lethargy I felt a year ago. The same fog in the head. I feel as if my mother has gone into her radiation session, but it isn't true. I've only been in this room for five minutes and I want to leave.

VII

I never thought of them as having faces or passions. I always imagined them with bodies and no heads; with a blur where their heads should be. I didn't even picture them with covered faces because I assumed that under the masks they sometimes wore on television there was something else. I imagined that they were interchangeable, like Lego figures with swappable torsos and legs. I couldn't imagine them playing cards or going to the market, though now that I've written this, I see them carrying bags of apples. As a girl, I called them Harry, and sometimes in traffic jams I shook a fist at the lights, saying: 'Turn green or I'm calling Harry.' It was many years later when I began to dream that my father was being killed or that I was their main target. The second nightmare was worse because of the loneliness, because I couldn't share my fears with anybody.

*

The name of the man who ordered the package bomb to be sent to my father was Miguel. I found this out by typing his nickname into Google. He's probably only called that by his family, or maybe not even by them. He's ten years older than me and he was born on the exact same day as my twin sisters, 6 July. I search for his nickname on a newspaper website and a few articles pop up. Many are illustrated with an image of his trial in early summer 2011 for sending a package bomb to my father in 2002. In the photograph he is raising one arm and biting his tongue as if trying to get my attention.

Nine years had gone by. In my family we no longer knelt by the car with a little mirror to check whether there was some explosive device wired to it. That time felt far away and hazy, like a movie from which one remembers only random details.

The day of the trial, some friends of my parents brought a bag of fresh fish to the apartment hotel across from the UN where my mother was staying. We wanted to make baked sea bass with white wine and lemon. Someone said in passing: 'Have you seen the picture in the paper?' and we said we had while we continued with the dinner preparations. My mother was tired. The effects of the chemo sessions were cumulative and she needed more sleep than usual. She could only have proteins for dinner and we had to work hard to come up with new things for her to eat. 'It was caught this morning,' my parents' friend said. I went down to the hotel café to borrow a few forks. The building was art deco and it must have had a glorious past, but now the rugs were frayed and the furniture was encrusted with dust. Still, it was cosy. Almost everyone who stayed there had some connection to the UN. Each week most of the guests were of a single nationality. One Monday they were all Italian, the next they were all Chinese, the next all Indian. We often ate fish and seafood, because Pisacane, the best fish market in Manhattan, was just a block from the hotel. There was good shopping in the area: rather expensive, but high quality. We bought our vegetables and fruit at the Amish Market, though my mother could hardly eat any of it. Her diet consisted of homemade hummus, hamburgers from P.J. Clarke's, lacquered duck from Peking Duck House, ravioli from Caffé Linda, and boiled lobster at ten dollars apiece from Pisacane.

*

17 January, 2002

It was my father's name on the package, but the address was my uncle's in Getxo. The postman reached the building around noon. The concierge looked through the mail, and when he saw who the package was for he said there was no one in the building by that name. The postman took the package, found a pen and was about to check the box for 'addressee unknown'. My cousin had just come into the lobby holding her nanny's hand. She was seven, blonde, and she stopped at the concierge's desk to watch the sorting of the mail. 'That package is for my uncle,' she said. 'Are you sure?' asked the mailman. 'Yes, that's his name,' she answered. My cousin stood waiting by the elevator with the package under her arm. The nanny was next to her. A neighbour on the second floor had taken her shopping up and was unloading the bags slowly.

A policeman came into the lobby and shouted: 'There's a bomb!' My cousin threw up her arms and dropped the package. The postman tossed the mail in the air; the letters hit the box with the bomb in it while my cousin's arms were still raised. Or at least that's how I imagine it.

For the following eight hours, I had no idea what was going on. I didn't hear from my parents. Later I would find out that they were at the opera. When the phone rang, I was preparing a presentation for an economics class at the university. At the other end of the line a woman spoke: 'The Minister of the Interior would like to offer your father his condolences.' 'What's happened?' I asked. The woman pretended not to have heard me and asked in a kind voice, 'Can your father come to the phone?' I told her that he wasn't home and hung up, not knowing what to make of the conversation. I searched for the name of the interior minister on the Internet and then my father's name. I saw the news. No one was answering the phone. As I finished the assignment, I reread the story on the computer. My parents got home around midnight. They came into the hall talking about Rigoletto and they told me what had happened that morning. 'If my number is up, it's up,' said my father. The next day, the bodyguard he would have from then on brought him a list of activities that he should avoid for safety's sake. These included: taking out money from cash machines, using public transportation, going to the news stand or the book store on our block, paying for parking, and walking anywhere.

The next morning I got up early to make it to class at eight. I took the Metro, and when I came out of the exit closest to the university, something happened that may have been real or that I may have dreamed. A young man in a leather jacket passed me and said: 'You were lucky.' Now, rereading the newspapers, I'm not sure whether my cousin's story is true, either. In front of me is an article that says that the package bomb was found in the post van.

*

I spend the morning googling Miguel, but hardly find anything. Apart from the photographs of the trial, there's a YouTube channel under his name and a feature in the magazine *Interviú* about his childhood and family.

The Miguel I find on the Internet doesn't scare me. I'm not frightened by the place where he seems to have lived for many years: 'The seventh floor of an apartment block with a view of the church of San Francisquito de Santutxu.'

Nor am I troubled by his parents, Ana and Josu, divorced in '98, when my family had been living in Madrid for three years. My grandfather Ricardo died that summer, so I guess '98 wasn't a good year for either family. Miguel's father worked for an electric company, his mother was an assistant at different shops. He also has a sister about whom I haven't been able to discover anything.

I find a YouTube account created by someone with the same name as him. I don't know whether it's real or fake. There are videos of Basque dancers and flamenco singers, Justin Bieber, Kraftwerk, the movie *Honey I Shrunk the Kids*, some Muppets sketches; clips of The Art of Noise, The Smiths, some reggae groups I don't recognise, a girl screaming, Luciano Pavarotti, video games, surfing videos, instructional videos showing how to play Metallica on the guitar and how to light a barbecue, gunmen, guerrillas, Adolf Hitler, Latin singers, and a comedy sketch in which two hooded figures fire three shots into a broken computer. None of the videos that I see scare me, but then I imagine Miguel in front of the computer and I can't describe what I feel.

Looking at pictures of him, I feel the same way I do when I look at images of cancer cells. I don't think about the threat, but about the story conjured up. The images of the tumours look like galaxies, and when I look at them, I tell myself stories about space. When I see Miguel sticking out his tongue and raising his arm at the trial for the package bomb he sent my father, I sense it isn't me whose attention he's trying to get.

VIII

When my mother came to New York for treatment, I was living in South Williamsburg, in Brooklyn, getting a master's degree in marketing from NYU, and I worked in the Times Square MTV building. Despite the overdose of neon outside the building, my office was a windowless, LED-less box. I remember that on my second day of work I googled 'no natural light in my office' and found a link to an Amazon listing for a little lamp that promised to solve my problem. According to the product description, thirty-five million Americans suffer from something called seasonal affective disorder, or SAD, and a University of Idaho study had revealed that in patients exposed to light for thirty to forty-five minutes a day, progress had been observed in the treatment of chronic depression, bipolar disorder, insomnia, bulimia, PMS and dementia. At the same university, another study had been conducted in which patients were divided into two groups, one given Prozac and the other exposed to forty minutes of light a day for a week. At this point in the article I wasn't surprised to read that it was the second group that had obtained better results.

The Friday after I found out about my mother's illness, I spent the day at home. I didn't work on Fridays, and I didn't have class, either. I usually managed to sleep until eleven and read in my pyjamas until lunchtime. That morning, however, the doorbell woke me up early. At the door, a messenger in a grey shirt handed me a package. I took it, signed a slip and thanked him. In the kitchen I got scissors and cut the tape. I stuck my hand into the styrofoam pellets and pulled out the lamp. It was an ugly, garish thing, three times bigger than I had imagined it would be. I plugged it in to check the quality of the light, which struck me as white and unpleasant. 'No returns', the box said.

I set the lamp on the floor, at the foot of the bed, and picked up my book again. That morning I was reading Walser's *The Walk*. As I was plumping my pillow, an image of the writer dead in the snow came into my head. I typed 'robert walser' into Google and clicked on Images; the first photograph in the second row was of his dead body. Footsteps in the snow led to the spot where he lay. His mouth was open and he had one hand on his belly and the other outstretched, reaching towards a hat. I began to read the first paragraph, looking up from the page to the photograph at each comma.

One morning, as the desire to take a walk came over me,
I put my hat on my head, left my writing room, or room of
phantoms, and ran down the stairs to hurry out into the street.

Robert Walser, 15 April, 1878–25 December, 1956. Buried in 2011
with three hundred thousand other photographs of himself in
Google Images.

In his book the writer goes out for a walk one morning in
1917. He must have done the same thing that Christmas Day,
almost four decades later. Perhaps he was sitting in his room
at the Herisau asylum, and though it had been years since he

gave up writing, he was projecting stories onto the white wall of his room; sitting in bed with his back to the window and stuck on some of his imaginary projections, he must have closed his eyes and wondered whether it would do him good to take a walk.

What I notice most about this photograph is the naive way in which it was taken. Some children playing in the woods come across the body. They circle the writer a few times and decide to call the police. The police arrive a few minutes later and proceed to photograph the body. I imagine a man putting film in the camera, turning the reel and backing up through the snow while looking through the viewfinder. Three or four steps away, the full complement of legs, arm and hat are inside the frame. The man presses the button and immortalises the body.

Today, almost a year and a half after reading the book, I'm still living in Brooklyn and still working in an office with no natural light, though not at the same company. Nor do I live in the same place, though I still have the lamp and the styrofoam pellets on the top shelf of a closet. Today is Sunday, 2 September, 2012. Normally on Sundays I write until I'm exhausted or until I run out of ideas. When it gets dark, I usually go to the cinema or take a walk. This afternoon the sound of glass breaking got me up from my desk. The bookcase in the living room had toppled over. On it there were some books, now scattered on the floor amid shards of glass and a wrecked record player.

I swept up the glass and stacked everything behind the sofa. While I was picking up the books I found Walser's *The Walk*. A small volume, ninety pages at most, with a plain white cover. I opened the book and read a paragraph that I had underlined in pencil.

> To lie here inconspicuous in the cool forest earth must be sweet. That one might still sense and enjoy death even in death! To have a grave in the forest would be lovely. Perhaps I should hear the birds singing and the rustling above me. I would like such a thing as that.

It occurred to me that perhaps Walser had stopped writing to focus his energy on making his wish come true. He must have chosen an asylum with a forest nearby, and each morning, before going out for a stroll, he must have put on his hat and taken an umbrella even if the sky was cloudless. On his walks he must have studied the lie of the land, paying special attention to the shape of the clearings and the height of the firs. I imagine Walser sitting on a stump, closing his eyes to listen to the branches rustling. Then he must have cleared the leaves from the ground with his umbrella and marked an X. Maybe that was where his body was found, I thought.

*

That summer I had learned to do a backwards dive into the pool. My toes were on the edge and my heels in the air, my back to the water and my eyes on a hedge growing through the cracks in the fence. I swung my arms a few times and pushed off, my spine arching and sending me into the pool fingertips first. I must have kept my eyes open, because as my body turned in the water I saw the upside-down image of a man sinking in a white cloud. My body kept turning. Stroking centimetres from the bottom and the west wall of the pool, I finally came up. Outside of the pool, people were crowding along the edge. A woman in a black bathing suit had jumped into the cloud. Now she emerged from it with her face dirty, hauling the body of the drowning man, who still had white stuff coming out of his mouth. The man had a gold crucifix around his neck that swung each time his head lost its perch and fell sideways.

I climbed up the stairs out of the water and saw the man lying in the grass. Next to him, a kid from the Red Cross was trying to revive him by pounding on his chest. But the man didn't move. He just lay there with his mouth open. Meanwhile, the woman in the black bathing suit was rinsing off in one of the showers by the changing rooms. Soon the pool was cordoned off with yellow tape. People had scattered, and near the body a woman and two girls stood holding each other. One of them was shivering and the other put a towel around her. The one who seemed to be the mother stared at the body, her lips parted in the same way as the man's. She stood there with her mouth open until the ambulance arrived. Some paramedics took the man away, covering him in a silver blanket, and the three women stood for a while longer by the pool, watching as the cloud dispersed.

*

I'd been trying to remember my mother, but I couldn't. For a few minutes I tried to reconstruct her face, but all I saw was black. Since the computer was in front of me, I searched her name on the Internet.

This appeared:

The first picture is her as a young woman, her hair parted on the side and falling over her shoulders. The rest of the pictures are images of gravestones. Marble, granite, flowers, no flowers, statuary. One is engraved with the shape of a heart and another with her last name, PASCH, in capital letters.

Suddenly I began to talk. I described my morning. The bookcase, the damage and the Walser book. 'Do you remember how much I liked my record player? Well, it's broken now.' Then I spent an hour staring at the screen trying to memorise her face.

It was then that I remembered the lamp. I took it down from the shelf and set it on my desk. When I plugged it in, the four LED tubes lit up and cast an ugly white light on my face.

Experience the incredible restorative capacity of our 10,000-lux therapy with negative ionizer. The Sun Touch Plus© lamp will bathe your face in natural light and release ions that brighten your spirits. Boost your mood, adjust your biological rhythms, and feel fresher, well-rested, and pampered with Sun Touch Plus©, the treatment recommended by psychologists all over the world.

IX

It wasn't long before my mother was trying to hide her illness. When we walked around Manhattan on days when she didn't have an appointment, she always tried to walk faster than me. If I told her that I needed to stop to rest, she insisted that we keep going. I don't think she did it consciously. If anyone had asked her whether she had cancer, she would have said yes. Still, each time someone asked 'How are you?' her answer was always 'Great.' It didn't matter that she might have spent the morning in the bathroom vomiting, or that the radiation therapy had made her sterile. Her reaction to illness was resistance. Nothing's wrong here. This isn't killing me. Look how well I am. Sometimes I even believed it myself.

Halfway through the treatment, she announced that she wanted to buy an apartment in Brooklyn. There was nothing I could do to stop her. The week that she had the chemo pump attached, she was already wandering around the neighbourhood where the apartment was and checking the price. She had visited the place twice with a friend and she couldn't stop talking about the views of Manhattan and the river from every room. We went back together to see it a few weeks later. During the subway ride she talked nonstop about the apartment and about family dinners overlooking the East River.

Meanwhile, I couldn't forget her illness. We visited the apartment. From the living room you could see all of Manhattan and the river full of cargo ships travelling up and down the waterway. A seaplane landed on the surface like a seagull, filled its tank with water and vanished. The girl from the real estate agency showed us around, but I could only look out. Then she started to talk about contracts. My mother wanted to close the deal as soon as possible and she asked me to help her with the paperwork. During the negotiations, no one mentioned her health. The closing day was the first time I thought my mother could die.

*

My family received a number of threats during the eighties, nineties, and the years after 2000. Until I was an adolescent, my parents managed to more or less shield me from it all, though I was aware that some of the things that happened to us were unusual. One morning, for example, someone tagged our house with a message that was hard to decipher or identify: a circle and a P, or maybe a half-R or half-B. Whoever was responsible for the graffiti had left it unfinished. Another day someone came in the dining room window. He threw a stone to break the glass and wandered around the room until the alarm went off, and then he was gone. In the summer of 1992 a man spent the whole night sitting in a white Ford Fiesta in front of our house. The engine was off, and every so often we could see a lit cigarette moving in the dark. My mother and I watched him through a window. We called the police. The man who spoke to us told us that the car was stolen and he said that some officers would be sent to arrest him, but by the time they arrived, the man with the cigarette had gone.

I found out about my grandfather's killing from a neighbour. I was seven. That day I came home crying and I told my parents what I'd heard. 'We didn't tell you before because you never asked us how he died,' my mother said. The two of them avoided giving me details about the kidnapping. Not long before, in '87 or '89, my father's little brother, my Uncle Cosme, committed suicide. Years later I learned that he had done it by pouring a can of gasoline over his head and setting fire to himself. Today I can't remember his face. Nor can I remember anyone looking sad, or any mention of his funeral or burial. There are just two stories I remember hearing about my uncle: that before he killed himself he spent weeks insisting that my mother go with him to the supermarket at El Corte Inglés, and that he was once caught shooting up heroin in our bathroom. I've never seen photographs of him, but in our living room there was a bronze figurine of a little girl in a walker, pleading to be lifted out. The piece had belonged to my uncle. It was a strange object, not pretty. The girl had a look of distress on her face.

*

A spring day in 1989

The Renault 4 stalled again on the hill between the train station and the church of San Ignacio. It was too steep a slope for such an old car. My mother and I got out, and, with the help of a man on the pavement, we tried to get it to start. She got back behind the wheel to turn the key while the man and I pushed from behind. The sound of the engine at first was like water coming to the boil in a pot, and then, a few minutes later, like the hum of a pressure cooker. I leaned my arms on the car, but I doubt the efforts of a five-and-a-half-year-old made any difference. The man dug the tips of his shoes into the road and pushed with his hands and the whole weight of his body. On the back of the car, on the hatch, there was a giant sticker of Mickey Mouse's face. I think one of my uncles gave it to my mother and she stuck it there because she thought I might like it. The car itself was a sight, yellow and beat-up; the Mickey Mouse face didn't look out of place. Normally the sticker was an object of pride for me, but that day my sweaty hands slipped on it. The wheels began to turn on their own, and the man and I celebrated our accomplishment by letting go of the car. My mother stopped the Renault and got out to thank the man, offering him a bottle of water from her bag. The man drank it. At the top of the hill were the grounds of San Ignacio, a park crossed by palm-lined paths that lay in front of the church. On the other side of the lawn, almost straight across from the beach overlook, was the nursery school. Some parents were waiting with their children on the benches for the doors to open. My mother waved to everybody and I imitated her. In English, I said 'Bye bye', and my mother replied, 'Bye bye Gabriela.'

*

Leaving Las Arenas, the landscape was leached of colour: the parks, beaches and freshly painted houses disappeared. This was the start of an industrial zone where concrete buildings sprouted, their balconies grimy from the smoke of the factories. Around Erandio, the water of the estuary was a yellowish grey, and each time that a ship went by it left a wake of soapy foam. In this neighbourhood the air was thick with the emissions from a number of chemical factories and the tall chimneys on the far side of the estuary. Every so often, some of the factories released fumes, and for fifteen minutes or half an hour their chimneys belched clouds of smoke. If you were driving, you had to roll up the windows as quickly as possible, and if you were out walking you had to cover your nose and mouth with a handkerchief and try to find shelter. Grass didn't grow in Erandio, and on the balconies of the buildings closest to the factories, the laundry got holey and dirty. As a girl I had no idea about any of this, but I remember that passing by in the car I worried that the white things hanging from the balconies would be soiled.

I imagine my mother driving into the centre of Bilbao, parking the car in the garage at El Corte Inglés and going into the supermarket there. She must have done a big shop. Then she must have had a sandwich at a bar on General Concha with a friend and got back in the car to return to Neguri.

I imagine that it was in Deusto, somewhere near the university, where my mother ran into a police checkpoint. Her Renault, yellow with a Mickey Mouse sticker on the hatch, must have stood out in the stream of traffic. There must have been lots of policemen, the sirens on their cars rotating silently and tinting the road orange. The officers, two by two, must have asked drivers for their papers, ordering them to pull off onto the hard shoulder by the estuary. One officer must have looked at the documents while the other, standing guard, kept his machine gun pointed at the driver. I imagine that when my mother passed through the checkpoint, a man gestured for her to pull over. She must have turned onto the shoulder, rolled down the window and greeted the officers. It wouldn't have been the first time that she had been stopped. What was unusual this time was that the policeman's gun was shaking. I imagine one of the officers saying slowly: 'Get out of the car now and put your hands on the bonnet.' My mother must have opened the door and stepped out, standing there for a second, smelling the sulphur of the factories and resting her palms on the bonnet. More officers must have arrived. One must have patted her down, two must have searched the car, and another two must have stood there with their rifles aimed at her. They must have pried up the seats, opened the glove compartment, slid their hands into every crevice. In the boot they must have found the grocery bags. They must have taken the things out one by one, leaving fruit, jam, cleaning products on the tarmac. I imagine one of the policemen with a mop in his hand saying: 'There's nothing here.' My mother, her hands still on the bonnet, must have sensed that the machine gun pointed at her ear wasn't shaking anymore. She must have relaxed too. The officer who'd had a hand on her back must have helped her straighten up. 'I'm sorry,' he must have said. I imagine my mother taking a deep breath and smelling the acidity in the air again. 'One of our fellow officers was just killed near here. We know that the shooter is in a yellow Renault 4 heading down the highway along the estuary . . . There aren't many cars like yours. And we know that the crime was committed by a woman.'

I imagine my mother getting back in the car, crossing the smoke cloud of Erandio again and heading to Neguri. Upon reaching our neighbourhood, the grass must have seemed too green and the houses too immaculate. My father was in India covering a conflict. She must have thought of him and missed him. I imagine my mother taking the groceries out of the boot, asking our long-time housekeeper María Jesús for help, and the two of them putting everything away in the refrigerator, the freezer and the pantry. My mother chose not to say anything to anybody about the incident, but she couldn't stop thinking about it. She must have felt watched. She must have passed the window and scanned the street, seeing no one but Raúl, the doorman of the building across the street, watering some plants. I imagine my mother going up to her room to call my grandfather. It always calmed her to talk to her father. 'Something just happened to me,' she must have said, and she must have told him the whole story, beginning with the car stalling on the hill and ending with the groceries that she had just unloaded in the kitchen. 'Don't worry,' my grandfather must have said, 'the police are aware of your situation.' I imagine my mother glancing at the clock. My father wouldn't call until night-time. Then she must have reread the postcard that he had just sent from Calcutta. 'I miss you and Gabriela so very very much.' My mother must have gone down the stairs and out to pick me up at the nursery school. Calle Marqués de Arriluce must have been empty. The abandoned house and the deserted mansion across the street must have looked more ominous to her than ever.

X

'She came into the house, took off her sun hat, opened the kitchen door and started to cry,' my sister Inés told me over the phone. The first cycle of chemotherapy ended in mid July, and it was common practice for the patient to spend six weeks without treatment to see how the disease progressed. The doctors advised my mother to go back to Spain and take a holiday, protecting herself from the sun but making sure to walk on the beach when it wasn't too hot. She was happy; the doctors were optimistic and everyone was sure that the tests scheduled for the end of the summer would show no trace of the disease. Before leaving for the coast she spent a week in Madrid. She felt strong, though every so often she needed to sleep at odd hours. It was four weeks before I could join her. I had to stay behind in New York to move into the new apartment in the tower block by the river.

The work on the kitchen of the apartment in Madrid began the same week that my mother discovered the lump and ended just before she got off the plane at Barajas, left her suitcases in her room, took off her hat and burst into tears at the sight of the renovated kitchen.

The job had taken longer than it was supposed to; no one had been keeping an eye on the workers. I remember that my sister

Inés, when she got back to Madrid after visiting my mother in New York, called me to say that she had found the workmen asleep on a sack of tiles.

Days after the renovation was finished, my sister realised that the door of the dish cupboard collided with the kitchen door, the water heater was too high, and the fuse box was hard to find, buried in the pantry. 'But if all the cupboards stay closed and we never blow a fuse, it's great,' she told me over the phone.

My mother didn't mention any flaws. She was satisfied with the new island, the new stove, the new countertop. In the kitchen, I think, she felt cured of the disease.

*

During the week she spent in Madrid, she had lots of energy. One afternoon she even went to IKEA to buy some stools for the kitchen counter. Things started to go downhill soon afterwards, the day she flew from Madrid to Cádiz.

When she boarded the plane at Barajas in the morning she was healthy, but forty-five minutes later, upon landing in Jerez, she hurried to the airport bathroom to vomit and she didn't feel well again after that. What surprised me most when I saw her three weeks later was her skin, damp and soft as gelatin. Her appearance in general was disconcerting. Sometimes she seemed very old and other times very young, her apparent age changing according to the angle or the time of day. She was as thin as she had been when she took me to school in the Renault 4, but her back was hunched and her skin was waxy. 'It's muscle pains', 'it's the side effects of the chemo' or 'everyone says you sweat a lot in menopause': this is what we told ourselves to keep believing that what was happening was normal. 'I'm fine, just fine,' my mother kept saying. For a month and a half we were adrift, hatching our own theories without seeing any doctor. Of the six weeks that my mother spent on vacation in Spain, I was in New York for four, moving and seeking reasons for her discomfort. I often thought about her father, my grandfather. He had died after his cancer metastasised to the bone. One day he sat down in a wheelchair and never got up again. According to what my family was telling me, it seemed that my mother had got worse. Still, she was walking. The day that she sat down and didn't get up was the day I would have to worry. Today, more than a year later, it occurs to me that maybe my mother had the same thought. Maybe that was why she refused to let us buy her a wheelchair and why she got angry whenever anyone mentioned metastasis. I think that was why she pretended it was her muscles that hurt, not her bones.

During her illness, time passed capriciously. I know it was six months because I can count the weeks from the time her treatment began until she died. When I got to Cádiz it scared me badly to see her, but I wasn't able to take in what was happening. Four weeks earlier, the doctors had told us that she would get better. I never considered the possibility that she was dying. In an email to a friend dated 10 August, 2011, I wrote: 'My mother is very weak, I think she's anaemic.'

*

The bird tree was in the middle of the golf course, by a pond. I was never there, but whenever I heard it mentioned I imagined a pine tree with lush branches and a bare trunk. My sister Inés told me that in the days before I got to Cádiz, she, Leticia and my mother had taken a stroll to the tree every evening. My mother could hardly walk, but she leaned on my sisters' arms until she reached the pond. The branches were full of all kinds of birds and the three of them watched their fluttering from below as the sun went down. My mother said that the walk did her good, but Inés remembers that she would get upset when her ankles gave way. One day she almost fell. Another day she needed to go to the bathroom halfway there, and my sisters had to help her hide behind a bush. My mother wanted to let go of them so they wouldn't have to see her crouch on the ground with her bottom in the air, but she wasn't able to support herself. When she rose, her hands were dirty and she tried to lean on my sisters without touching them. Inés said it was hard to hold her up, that she was nervous and her legs shook.

Every evening, after walking to the tree, my mother took off her shoes, lay down in bed and asked someone to draw the curtains. When I got to Cádiz that's where she was, lying on the bed barefoot in the dark.

*

My father took a hand towel and soaked it in the basin that he had put next to the bedside table. He sank his arm into the basin up to the elbow and swished the towel a few times before wringing it out and draping it over his wife's forehead. On the mattress, my mother sweated and arched her back. She said that putting weight on the crown of her head helped her bear the ache in her muscles. Sometimes, when the stretches worked and she was able to relax, she would open and close her lips, breathing in. 'If I take deep breaths, maybe my body will cool down faster.'

'Don't worry,' my father said as he stroked her face, 'this must be a side effect of the chemo.' Then he rubbed her arms, her lower thighs, and her legs from knee to ankle. Her skin was shiny and wet, so that his hand slid easily, smoothing the hairs to her body.

Every day she looked more like a narrow-hipped adolescent. Her hair had grown, and now it fell eight inches below her shoulders. He was sitting on the bed beside her, stroking her head. Every so often he tangled his index finger in a lock of hair, straightening the wavy strands. I imagine he must have thought how long it had been since he saw her hair like this.

XI

On the morning of 21 August, 2011, we left Cádiz, and on the
night of the 22nd we landed in New York. My mother's whole
body hurt. The next day we had an appointment with the oncologist, but we didn't want to wait and we went straight to the
hospital. It was raining. From the window of the plane all you
could see were blurs of light. My mother said that she wanted
an ambulance for the ride into Manhattan, but I managed to
convince her that we should take a taxi. The idea of waiting
filled me with dread, and anyway, I didn't know what you had
to do to get an ambulance. The taxi moved along the highway
and the blurs of light grew. So much rain was coming down
that it seemed like winter. She didn't complain. When we got
to the hospital, the taxi driver helped me unfold the wheelchair
while holding an umbrella over my head. I lifted my mother
and sat her in the chair, and the driver walked us to the recep-
tion desk. I went back for the luggage and left it at the desk. We
went up to the emergency room. I was soaked; my mother was
dry. They put us in an examination room. I told her that I had
bought a blender and I was going to make her lots of juices. 'Has
the cancer metastasised?' a nurse asked. I said that it hadn't. The
nurse left and I started to talk about smoothies. A young doctor
came in. After he had introduced himself, he took a wooden

tongue depressor out of a box and stepped over to put it in her mouth. Two hours of tests. They couldn't say what she might have in addition to cancer. Maybe some sort of virus? When they saw the sores in her mouth they thought it might be AIDS. 'But how is that possible?' my mother kept saying. It was past midnight when they sent us to a room on the fifteenth floor. The results wouldn't be in until the next day. I went with my mother to her new room, we talked for a while, and after yawning a few times I took a taxi home with the suitcases.

*

Room 1539 had light-coloured walls and a window. In the upper-right corner hung a TV that we hardly ever turned on. Besides the television, there were four pieces of furniture: a bed, a bedside table, a recliner, and the wooden trolley on which meals were served.

On the right-hand wall there were various machines and some IV bags hanging from a metal pole. You had to duck between them to get into the bathroom, a tiny cubicle with a chair standing on the shower tray.

The hospital rules required visitors to protect themselves from patients who might be contagious, and since it wasn't yet clear whether my mother had a virus or not, before coming into the room you had to put on a gown, a cap and a mask, and scrub your hands with gel from a dispenser on the wall.

The first morning that I went to see my mother I followed the procedure: I put on the green paper clothes and I scrubbed my hands. When I came into the room I found her in bed tapping on a hardboiled egg with the edge of a spoon. When she had swallowed the yolk, she asked me to please help her shower.

Up until now she had always done it herself. Despite her weakness and my attempts to prevent her, in Cádiz she had found the strength to go into the bathroom and wash. While the water was running, I would sit by the door until the dripping stopped. Then I would creep slowly away from her room, sit in the living room and pretend that I had been watching TV or reading a magazine.

That morning in the hospital her request for help took me by surprise. It didn't occur to me to call anybody. I put my arm around her and helped her to sit up. She tired easily. We stopped for a few minutes so that she could catch her breath. When her breathing steadied, I lifted her legs and moved them carefully until they were dangling off the bed. Then we rested a while longer. We proceeded like this, little by little, until she managed to stand and walk slowly to the bathroom. When she reached the shower she stopped, raised her arms and waited for me to undress her. I undid her gown and threw it into a bin, then I pulled her paper panties down by the elastic.

The last time I had seen my mother naked I was very small. One day my parents were careless and I opened the door to the bathroom and found them with no clothes on under the water. All I could make out at first was a vague outline, but in a struggle for the shower head the curtain fell open and I saw them clinging frenziedly to each other with a ton of suds on their heads.

When I turned on the shower at the hospital, my mother was standing on the tiles, facing the water, with her back to me. I was afraid that she would turn around. The radiation had affected the whole lower part of her body, and I thought her sex would be red, black or burned.

To my surprise, it wasn't. It looked young and smooth, seemingly intact. The look of it matched the rest of her adolescent shape. I asked her to sit on the little chair on the shower tray. She sat. I asked her to hold the shower head while I looked for the soap. She held it. But her attention slid to the tiles and when I returned with the gel I found water pooling on the floor.

I washed my mother's face, neck and chest. My green paper gown got wet and the mask stuck to my tongue. I finished washing her body and her hair and I looked around for a towel but there weren't any in the bathroom. I asked my mother to hold the shower head again and this time I was careful to aim the spray at her body. I went out into the corridor in my wet gown. I approached a nurse. When I spoke behind the mask I breathed in my own breath.

The nurse raised her voice when she saw me in the paper gown in the hallway. She made me take it off. She scolded me for risking the health of others with the possible viruses in the room. Then she showed me the cupboard where the towels were kept. At the door to the room I put on a new cap, mask and gown.

The pool had spread. My mother was still sitting on the chair with her eyes on the tiles, her gaze lost. The spray twisted at her feet on the shower floor. When I came in she greeted me happily. I asked whether she was cold. She said no. I turned off the water, put a towel around her shoulders and hugged her. When she felt the contact of my skin she stiffened, looked around and said, 'This is a mess, isn't it?' 'A little,' I said. I helped her up. She stood there again in the shower with her arms raised, but I convinced her to go back into the room, pushing aside the IV bags for her. I finished drying her. I got a clean pair of panties and I knelt down on the floor. First I lifted one foot and pulled the underwear over her left ankle, then I lifted the other foot and repeated the motion. Once both legs were in, I pulled the panties up until the elastic was around her waist. Then, one by one, I got her arms into the sleeves of the nightgown, an open gown that closed at the back with three white ties. I tied them and helped her to lie down on the bed.

There was a hair dryer in the drawer of the bedside table. I turned it on and pointed it at her face. She closed her eyes. When I was done I brushed her hair, put moisturiser on her and did her make-up. When the nurse came into the room she saw her and said: 'She looks like a diva.'

*

The morning hours of 23 August were peaceful. After the shower, my mother and I spent a while talking about the summer, though sometimes she would fall silent abruptly, look at me and say: 'As if I could possibly have AIDS.' It was around twelve that things started to get complicated. Shortly after noon, a big Latino doctor whom we'd met for the first time that morning came into the room. In his hand he had a little blue plastic glass with a red carnation in it. He sat on the edge of the bed, took paper and a pen from the pocket of his gown and drew a liver with a hole in it and fireworks coming out. Then he explained what *silent metastasis* meant and he told us that the cancer had spread to the liver, the kidneys, the lungs and the bones. When he had finished talking, he looked at us a few times to see whether we'd understood what he was saying. I nodded. My mother didn't. The doctor gave my mother the little blue glass with the carnation in it and told us that next week he was moving hospitals to Mount Sinai. The two of us smiled when he told us this, wishing him luck and waving goodbye, and when he left, we sat there for a while staring at the carnation and the glass, trying to find some explanation.

Around one, a friend came to visit me. When she saw my mother and I staring at the glass, she joined us in contemplation, but after a while she said that she was hungry. Her revolt shook me from my daze and we went to get a sandwich. While we were on our way to the deli the earthquake hit. A tremor of magnitude 5.9 on the Richter scale was rocking the east coast of the United States. Outside we didn't feel it, so I talked on, oblivious of tectonic plates, and my friend smoked, indifferent to the movements of the earth. In Washington the Pentagon was being evacuated, the airports had just been closed, and the foundations of Manhattan's skyscrapers shuddered, knocking over the coffee cups of office workers. Still, the only tremor that I felt that afternoon was in my head. After we had eaten we went back to the room. My mother told us that the bedside table had moved and that during one of the shocks the plastic cup and the carnation had flown over the bed. 'Thank God I don't have to look at them anymore.'

*

After my friend left, my mother called my father to give him the news. She was sitting on the bed with her legs drawn up. In one hand she held the phone and with the other she pleated the bedspread.

'Hello, Enrique,' said my mother, 'the doctor was just here.'

There was a silence.

'He says the tumour has broken out and spread to the rest of my body.'

There was another silence.

'And he says he's not surprised that my back hurts because I have three broken vertebrae.'

My mother glanced over towards the recliner where I was sitting and asked me to get her a piece of paper and a pencil. She wrote down a number. Then she said: 'Yes, come quickly, please, I love you so much,' and when she hung up she left the phone on the bed and was silent.

*

Her first reaction was to fall apart. But then she reflected and let it be known that she was glad no one had hidden what was happening from her. She found acceptance in the time it took her to eat the yoghurt on her meal tray. Which makes me suspect that maybe her unconscious already knew that she was going to die. I was calm too. My reaction to the news was nothing like what I'd imagined: no wild religious fervour, no agony. All I felt like was sitting next to her and talking.

I don't think I broke the news gently to my sisters. 'This is it, get to Madrid as fast as you can and I'll find flights for you.' They cried a lot. They were on the beach, their hair wet, surrounded by people. One of them had the outbreak of religiosity that I had feared and she started to talk to me about miracles. My other sister didn't know what to say and was silent for minutes at the other end of the line. The next day everyone arrived: my father on one flight and my sisters on another. My father couldn't handle any paperwork and he was incapable of talking to the insurance company or the bank. Sometimes he wept. Other times he said strange things like 'I saw the blood-stained rosary'. My mother was the only one who was able to soothe him.

*

Today is 23 October, 2012

After getting out of the elevator on the fifteenth floor, I wasn't able to go straight to my mother's old room. Instead, I headed to the patients' lounge by the elevators. Now I'm sitting here, writing. In the room, two nurses carry fresh carnations back and forth and an Indian-American couple hold hands. The woman bows her head and the man squeezes her fingers hard.

The nurses with their arms full of flowers have gone into a glassed-in space with an array of tools and cups. On the table there are thirty blue cups in rows. The women in white gowns with their sleeves rolled up take the carnations one by one, clip their stems and set them in the cups.

On the wall across from me is an activity calendar drawn with a broad-tipped marker. It looks like it was made by someone with an unsteady hand, because there are hitches and jags in the lines. I wonder whether the person who drew it is dead already. This is the place patients come to avoid thinking: they paint pottery, arrange flowers and talk about the past. I imagine a woman with grey hair making the calendar, tracing her marker along the edge of a ruler and then forgetting that she has it in her hand.

I stop looking around and I get up to visit Room 1539.

I've come home.

Through the glass in the door I recognise the Indian woman from the lounge. She's sitting in the recliner by the bed, her defeated body slumped forwards and her forehead resting on her arms. Of the patient I can't see much. Just a dark, wrinkled foot. I don't dare come any closer to the door to see more; I could do it with the excuse of using the hand sanitiser on the wall, but I keep walking along the hallway. At the door to the next room I see a bed with a body in it covered by a sheet. It looks like a man. There is no family with him. He's there, going nowhere, waiting for someone to collect him.

I keep walking on into the bathroom because I don't know where to go. I step inside and spend a while standing there without using the toilet. I'm filled with anxiety and I turn on the tap to wet my wrists.

Then I come out of the bathroom and walk the hallway some more. This time I do see the face of the patient lying in the room. On the trip from the hospital back to my apartment I think about how many people must have died in the same bed over the past year. I consider the processes, the protocols, the eight weeks of radiation and the eight weeks of chemo. I calculate percentages: 56 per cent of patients with the same type of cancer survive, 43 per cent of surgeries have a successful outcome. 'You'll live to see your grandchildren,' said Doctor Marsden at our first appointment.

XII

New Yorkers talk more about death than anyone else in the Western world because on 11 September, 2001, they all thought they might die. The crater at Ground Zero has been there for more than ten years, and there are still ads in the subway offering assistance to people with post-traumatic stress or respiratory problems. The doctors here don't lie. If they think you're going to die, they say: 'You're dying.' After that, a psychologist comes into the room and the patient recounts the most intimate details of her life very quickly, because there isn't much time.

A few hours after we learned that my mother's disease had spread throughout her body, a Venezuelan woman with a very round face knocked at the door of her room. 'Hello, I'm the hospital psychologist,' she said to me. 'Would you mind leaving me alone for a while with the patient?' 'Sure, that's fine,' I replied and I left the room. After I had closed the door I stood there for a while watching through the glass. My mother was sitting Indian-style. The psychologist had her back to me. I sat on a little bench in the hallway and waited for them to finish talking.

Half an hour later the psychologist came to the door and invited me in. 'You're Gabriela, right?' she asked. 'Yes,' I replied.

'My name is Susana,' she said, adjusting her glasses and looking from my mother to me. 'Your mother told me that during her illness you walked a lot.' 'Yes,' I said, and I imagined my mother from behind, among the cherry trees on Stuyvesant Street. 'All we had left to see was Brighton Beach,' said my mother.

*

25 October, 2012

I'm sitting on a wooden bench across from the beach. The sky is overcast but there's a hole above the pier through which light streams down to the water. The sand is clean, a pale, faded yellow. This is a city beach where seagulls live alongside pigeons.

Behind me, between my left shoulder and my right shoulder, is Café Moscow. On its terrace, seven Russians in tracksuits are playing chess, singing Bolshevik songs, eating paninis, soup and hot dogs, and drinking soda. On the bar radio 'The Internationale' is playing, and every once in a while the Russians sing along to the verses they know.

It's 10.43 a.m. in the New York neighbourhood of Brighton Beach, a place situated on a spit of land that seems to want to detach itself from the south of Brooklyn. I got here by train. First I took the L and then I changed to the Q at Union Square, where I waited a while for the train, uncomfortable, my buttocks resting on a cold bench with protruding nail heads. A Caribbean woman in a bright turban sat down next to me. She looked as if she had just got off the plane from Trinidad. The woman took a deck of white index cards ruled in red from her pocket, chose one at random, and wrote in capital letters: CULTURE SHOCK.

Then my train came and I got on. For the first five minutes of the trip I wondered what the woman would write on the rest of her cards.

I've come to Brighton Beach to see what it's like. After walking some of its streets, I can say that it's a terrible neighbourhood. It's ugly and full of the lame and the infirm. Old people pushing Zimmer frames and fat men in wheelchairs move along the boardwalk. As I write these words I'm glad my mother never came here.

XIII

On 27 and 28 August, Hurricane Irene touched down on the east coast of the United States. On the 26th our building was evacuated, and on the night of the 27th the eye of the storm passed over the city of New York.

The morning of the 26th I ate breakfast while playing with an interactive map on the front page of the *New York Times* website. When I rolled the mouse over the streets on my block, a blinking red marker indicated that our building was in an evacuation zone. I soon got an email from Peter Ujkej, the superintendent. The message was titled 'Evacuation Alert', its tone at once polite and alarmist. In it, the super asked residents to vacate their apartments. A list of tasks was attached: bring in terrace furniture, shut off power, protect fragile objects from wind gusts, make sure windows are closed tight and don't leave pets at home alone. I got my father and sisters out of bed, and, among the four of us, we put things in order. In the lobby, Peter was stacking sandbags around the doorjambs.

The street was full of people carrying pillows, rucksacks and dogs. We got on the subway at the Bedford Avenue stop and crossed under the East River. Forty minutes later we emerged from the subway exit nearest the hospital. On the stairs we saw a poster that read: 'Public transportation will be suspended from 4 p.m. today (08/26/2011) until further notice.'

In Room 1539 my mother was watching a documentary on the life of Jackie Onassis. Now she only liked soft, cold food and she was eating gelatin from a bowl. She was so focused on the life of the First Lady that when we came in she shushed us: 'They're going to talk about the White House years now.' Then there was a break for a hurricane update and the screen filled with weather maps. I thought that the eye of the storm looked a lot like my mother's colon.

From the window of the room we watched the sky grow dark and the wind rise. My parents, my sisters and I talked, looking out every so often to gauge the intensity of the storm. My mother clutched her liver as she told us how she had met our father. We spent the hurricane talking, she in a chair with her feet up and the rest of us gathered around her. My father wrote down everything she said in a notebook. Sometimes he asked her questions. I did some writing, too, on the back of a receipt that was in my bag. And then I lost it. Maybe I threw it away by mistake. It had been a long time since we were all together: my sisters and I lived in three different countries. It was strange, I thought, that my parents had never told us these stories about their courtship.

*

Two days after the hurricane there was no trace of the storm: no fallen trees or traffic snarls. Public transportation gradually started up and planes were taking off and landing at the airports again. My parents left for Madrid on the first flight out of JFK. My sisters and I had to come in stages. Two days later for them, and three for me, via Charlotte.

My mother had needed to prepare herself for the trip. Gather strength. She wanted to see her friends and the rest of the family, and die in Madrid. The day before the flight, my father, my sister and I went out with her into the hallway by her room so she could make a few rounds with the walker. We went back and forth three times. Then, after she was put into bed, she was given a little tube with a white ball to blow into. The nurse prepared a transfusion. She hung two bags of blood from a stand and connected them to my mother's arm. As the liquid was distributed around her body, her wrinkles filled and her lips regained their colour. She grew younger. Her face was the same as it had been when we lived in Neguri. She wore a fuchsia dress, I was six, and the sun fell on us from the side.

My mother constantly googled what was happening to her. Types of cancer, 'Madrid ambulance'. She gave us advice: 'Live lightly', 'I want Handel at my funeral'.

The suitcases were packed a day early. Doctor Spring came to say goodbye. 'You were doing such a good job,' she said. 'Well,' my mother said, 'how was Italy?' Doctor Spring wiped a tear away with two fingers and said, 'Sardinia is just as pretty as I remembered it.' 'Italy is lovely,' replied my mother. The nurse came into the room pushing a wheelchair. My mother was ready to go. We had dressed her in a long blue skirt and a sun hat. We helped her into the chair and went down to the lobby. The ambulance was parked at the front door of the hospital. Two men put her on a stretcher in the ambulance and I sat next to her. My father and my sisters followed behind, in a taxi. My mother looked out the window and I watched her.

*

In an email to my flatmate just before landing in Madrid, my mother wrote: 'I'm sorry I won't be seeing you again. It was a wonderful trip!'

XIV

My mother lost consciousness in the middle of the afternoon on 3 September, 2011. She was sitting in bed, looking at me, when her left eye began to quiver. My sister Inés and my great aunt were with me at the head of the bed. My mother's neck spasmed. Her mouth filled with foam. Everyone stared at her in silence, except for me. As my mother was convulsing, I was doubled over by an attack of nervous laughter. Maybe my subconscious wanted my body to move like hers, to lose control at the same time. I think my sister Inés understood. My great aunt gave me a bewildered look. My mother's consciousness was vanishing and mine wanted to flee.

'Where is she?' my sister Leticia asked me a little later. 'She isn't there,' I answered, pointing to the body on the bed. What made my mother my mother had disappeared in the attack. She had spent the morning sleeping, scarcely moving, but you could feel her presence. That afternoon, after her eyes quivered, it was gone. She was breathing, but she wasn't there.

I wanted to photograph the room. Open the drawers and the cupboards to take pictures of what was inside. In the end I didn't do it. I pulled back the curtains and looked out at the mountains on the horizon. The room had been kept dark, but now I needed the light to come in. I put all her things away in a rucksack: two nightgowns, the outfit she'd worn on the plane, her toothbrush, her eau de cologne and her moisturiser. My mother's appearance was unnerving: propped up in bed, breathing as if she were drowning, there was pus between her eyelids and she got thinner with each breath. We had to keep her company until she was gone. Sometimes I felt like I was in the waiting room of some random doctor, sitting in a chair staring at a poster of Van Gogh's sunflowers. As she was dying my wisdom teeth started to come in and I looked at photographs of a trip we took together to Chile, to remember her when she was alive. My mother died between 3 and 4 a.m. on Tuesday, 6 September, 2011. My father and some of his siblings were with her. Her three daughters were asleep at home. We knew she would die that night, but for us it had already been three days since she stopped existing. My father and my aunt rang the bell early that morning and I went down to let them in. They told me how it had happened. I don't remember whether there were tears. I had spent days imagining the moment. Each night I would see some family weeping in the waiting room over the same catalogue of coffins from the funeral home and think that soon we would be the ones looking at it. The day before, I had asked my father to take charge of organising the funeral and the burial. I couldn't do it. The next morning, my father and his oldest sister sat down on the sofa in the waiting room to choose the coffin.

XV

'I've been here before,' my father must have thought. I thought it, anyway. I had been here before, in the same room of the Tres Cantos funeral home, my feet on the same yellow marble floor, with the same dazed expression on my face. My mother's body in the same place that my grandmother's had been. The same joke about the *Memorial Diamonds: gems created from a loved one's lock of hair.* More dazed this time. Though the room was full of people, I had eyes only for my father, my sisters and the box with my mother in it. 'Do you want to see her?' my father asked. 'I'd rather not,' I answered. Then he told me that they had dressed her in a blue tunic, the same colour as the trousers that she used to wear to paint furniture. He talked to me about my grandfather's body: 'I saw it,' he said. At the time I didn't pay much attention, but now I think I understand how important it was for him to see his dead father. It helped him to stay sane. To acknowledge that what had happened was real. My father wanted me to see my mother so that I could handle her death better. I didn't want to. I don't regret it now, because the last time I saw her, she had already stopped existing.

*

21 August, 2013,

Santo Ángel de la Guarda Municipal Cemetery,

Pozuelo de Alarcón, Madrid

A man with a bucket of water in his right hand and a flat cap strolls among the graves in the cemetery. It's sunny and the light strikes him full on, so that now and then, despite the cap, he holds his hand up like a visor to shield his face. The man stops in front of a headstone and empties the water from the bucket on it. Then he takes a rag out of his back pocket, sprinkles it with cleaning fluid and scrubs the stone. I watch him as I write on a laptop that warms my thighs. I'm leaning on a granite slab polished by Crespo de Alcorcón Marble Co. Buried underneath it are my mother and my maternal grandparents. The family grave is clean and dry, so I assume that the man with the bucket won't come by. It's nine in the morning and there's lots of activity in the cemetery. The caretaker greeted me a while ago, next to an orange digger in which he now rolls along a nearby path. When he sees me sitting on the stone he waves and I stop writing for a second to wave back.

Flies buzz around me. At the mausoleum of the Cantero Núñez family, a bee rubs against a branch, making a noise like a cricket. The man in the orange digger passes me again, climbs down and says: 'When you're ready to leave, you should go out the back gate, it's closer.'

'Your first time here, isn't it?' he'd asked when he saw me come into the cemetery with the laptop under my arm. 'Yes,' I replied. Then he told me how to find my mother and led me part of the way.

I thought the grave was to the right of the main entrance and it turns out that it's to the left. I thought the grave was on the edge of a path, and it turns out that it's in the middle of a section. Now, typing here on the slab, it's strange to me that I feel so little. I don't sense any strange presence and I'm not sad, just a little upset about having no small change to buy flowers from the vending machine at the entrance: 'Refrigerated bouquets. No credit cards or notes larger than twenty euros.'

I talk constantly about my mother, but today I'm having a hard time remembering her. Maybe because it's all so remote. Or at least it isn't any easier here than in the middle of some ordinary task, like trimming beans for dinner. I make an effort. I remember that the day of the burial I stood to the right of the grave, not to the left as I had imagined it. That morning there was a hearse, a pine box, and a cement mixer that kept turning. I remember the sound of the cement mixer very well. The worker with the bucket, the man with the orange digger, or maybe someone else, scooped up a shovelful of cement and tossed it in the hole while the rest of us pulled flowers from the wreaths and threw them in. The sun was very hot. Like today. The sun and the sweat are the only things that are like what I remember. What isn't the same is the smell. That morning I was wearing a black dress that I'd taken from my mother's wardrobe. It hadn't been washed, and when I began to sweat, the oils of the fabric mingled with mine. Everything started to smell like her. My mother and I, burying my mother. It's only now, imagining her scent, that I feel her nearby.

XVI

On 7 September, 2011, three obituaries appeared in the paper. At first I couldn't understand why my mother's death was of interest to the press. Then I was frustrated, because some of the reflections shared had nothing to do with the way I remembered her. I tried to say something about her that would satisfy me, but I couldn't. When I tried to get to the heart of who she was, everything I wrote seemed irrelevant. My ideas changed by the day or according to circumstances. Sometimes I was sad, because I felt that I hadn't been able to encompass her nuances. I thought that maybe it was a problem of length. My mother wasn't three paragraphs long, or six.

*

My mother was warmth and presence. Goodness and light. My mother was many of the things that are said about the dead, but in her case they were all true.

*

In the book *National Politics in Vizcaya*, written by my grandfather in 1947, there is a prologue that reflects briefly on the relationship between private life and politics in my family. Towards the end of the seventies, all of Vizcaya's positions of power were occupied by members of ten or twelve families. I belong to one of those families. The author of the prologue, Rafael Sánchez Mazas, believes it's inevitable that the history of the families be identified with the history of the province.

> My dear Javier, I cannot help but allude to long-distant yet still immediate family memories in speaking of your book [...] because, among other things, it is undeniably a book of family memories. 'How can this be?' some reader with no knowledge of Basque life and history will ask. All one can do is answer simply: 'Because it was.' [...] Whereas in all of Spain and nearly all of Europe politics gradually became a politics of the individual, in Vizcaya everything was a politics of the family.

Now, after having spent months in the archives reading my grandfather's story, I understand that the symbolic value of Neguri and my last name still endures. My private life is still political. And so is my mother's death. The language, the silences, the houses, the small tensions of living together, the feelings... It's all political. Even literature. The fact that one of my favourite books as a child was *La vida nueva de Pedrito Andía* is political. My father's tone while reading me Machado's 'The Evergreen Oaks' before bedtime is political: 'Who has beheld without trembling / a stand of beeches in a pinewood?' He always stressed those lines. As I write about my family, I reread Machado and I repeat the poem frequently. I imagine my mother and grandfather as evergreen oaks (simple, strong, free of torment).

A month and a half after my mother died, on 20 October, 2011, ETA announced a final halt to armed conflict.

XVII

Like most skating rinks, this one was rectangular, and it was in the middle of a park. The surface was artificial ice and it was kept hard by a machine that made a constant noise like a fan. I can't remember exactly why we decided to go there. I think my mother saw an ad in the paper with a picture of the rectangle surrounded by snowy hedges and thought it would be a nice Sunday plan. We rented skates in an iron and glass palace that smelled like wet socks. My parents and two other couples sat in the café overlooking the rink. My sisters and four friends put their skates on with me, then headed in a pack out of the changing room and onto the ice.

When I had finished tying my laces, I got up and walked slowly to the rink, digging my skate blades into the stone, before gliding into the crowd. I went around a few times. The fourth time, a waiter with a black bow tie brought drinks to my parents and their friends: six cups, a teapot, a coffee pot and a little jug of milk. On my next lap I saw my mother lift a cup to her lips, the red tag of her rooibos tea dangling. As I kept skating I remembered a recurring dream that I'd had again the week before. My family and I were landing one Friday morning at Heathrow Airport, and as we waited for our suitcases, a man with a piercing voice shouted through a megaphone: 'Bomb alert! Bomb alert!' Chaos was unleashed. Frenzied crowds swarmed around the room, looking for a way out. On the other side of the belt, my father grabbed his suitcase and vanished, pushing a trolley. A policeman with a whistle herded us all out onto the runway. We walked among planes and buses until we came to an empty car park where we spent an hour going in circles as if on a skating rink. My mother kept asking: 'Where's your father? Do you see him, Gabriela?' The nervous crowd waved and shouted at a policeman who remained inscrutable in the face of their insults. The rest of us kept looping around the perimeter of the car park.

At the ice skating rink I watched my father drinking coffee. He looked calm. But as relaxed as he seemed, I thought he might be ready to jump up and run out. He talked to his friends and laughed. He put his arm around my mother and watched us circle the ice.

At the end of my dream the policeman got tired of searching for bombs, and my mother and I were reunited with my father at an Italian restaurant. He was eating spaghetti with his napkin tucked into his shirt and he smiled, his teeth red with sauce: 'There you are! I'm so glad you're all right,' he said before raising the fork to his mouth. My mother and I sat down and ordered two plates of pasta. I felt a great urge to scream, but I didn't.

*

There were four pairs of black shoes lined up under the desk, heels together. The neatness of the row stood in contrast to the untidiness of the room: piles of newspapers on the chair, the dresser and one side of the bed. My father picked up a shoe and polished it with a baby wipe.

During my mother's illness, my father and I had to get to know each other again. I'm not sure when we lost touch. Sometimes I think it was the day I banned him from my room, forbidding him to read me any more bedtime poems. 'I'd rather read on my own,' I said, and he vanished down the hallway with a volume of the verse of Catullus under his arm.

Ever since I'd been living in New York, we'd hardly talked. 'I didn't want to bother you,' he said one day. Meanwhile, I never felt the need to find an excuse. It was his responsibility as a father to seek me out, I thought, and mine, as the daughter, to try to escape his control.

Some days I felt distant from my family, but other days I worried that I was too independent. Still, when my mother got sick, I realised that my father, my sisters and I had got used to being apart because she bridged the gap.

A wipe stained with shoe polish lay on the floor. My father took another pair of shoes and turned them over to check the state of the soles. He lingered over the scuffs; he contemplated the unequal distribution of the weight of her body. He took a clean wipe from a blue container and one by one he rubbed the little folds sewn along each side of the instep. There was no tension, no sound, just my father's hand smoothing the leather.

*

The week after my mother died, my father rearranged the furniture and art in our house. One day he piled all of his wife's clothes on the mattress, loaded everything into the boot of his car and took it to his office. Another day he brought two portraits out of storage and hung them over the sofa in the living room. In one of them my mother is wearing a green dress and has her hands hidden behind her. On the canvas, her eyes slant like my sister Inés's. That night, my father asked Inés to please sleep in the same room with him.

When I think about my mother's illness it's hard for me to remember my father. All I get are flashes. My father laying cold washcloths on my mother's forehead. My father writing in a notebook, taking down everything that she said at the hospital. Otherwise, most of my memories are of me and my mother. My picture of him sharpens three days before her death, when I began to feel weak and he made all the decisions about palliative care and the burial. Sometimes, he talked about my grandfather. He compared the two deaths. It surprised me.

In my family there were familiar stories that we told about my father. There was the story that he was hung up on security precautions and the story that he talked too much about the family's past. Sometimes, when he brought up one of these subjects, we would give him a baffled look, as if there were no danger and as if our last name was of no consequence. Now I think I didn't listen to him much during my mother's illness. When he told me he was afraid that she was dying, I thought he was exaggerating.

*

Until we moved to Madrid, my father fantasised about shedding his social class, about being the son of a cook or a nanny and running wild in the fields of Kanala. As an adolescent I had the same wish. I thought that what happened in other neighbourhoods was much more interesting than what happened in ours. I walked along Calle del General Ricardos de Carabanchel, imagining that this was where people lived who had read the same books and listened to the same music as me. When my father dreamed of life in the country, he yearned for its freedom and simplicity.

When my mother died, I was essentially the same age my father had been when my grandfather was killed. He was twenty-nine; I was twenty-eight. Both of us were living in New York.

*

My father is the opposite of my mother. My mother was a feather. My father is a concrete block that wishes it were a feather. My mother left little trace and travelled by bus. My father couldn't move without a security detail. My mother let the past go. My father is always aware of the family history.

My father wasn't able to loosen up until after my mother's death. In October 2011 ETA stopped killing and in 2012 he was able to give up his bodyguard. During the mourning period he grieved for his wife, but he also enjoyed more freedom. He lost weight. He started to do some things that my mother never let him do: work from his bedroom, walk shirtless from his room to the kitchen for water. Yesterday he called me and said that he wanted to start writing again.

＊

I hadn't read anything my father wrote until this summer. One night, when we were sharing a room in a country house near Santander, he went out for dinner with a friend and I stayed home alone. Wandering around the room in my nightgown, I caught sight on the bedside table of a volume of the book that he has spent half a lifetime writing, in a plastic ring binder. I opened it and read some bits. I was afraid that it would disappoint me, but it didn't, even though most of the chapters were in pieces. I read a passage about Regina, a friend of my father's whom I met as a child. Regina lived in a red house on Ereaga Beach with a dog cemetery in the garden. The English names of her pets and the pets of deceased family members were chiselled on tiny tombstones. The graveyard was surrounded by a wooden fence in a garden that sloped down to the sea. One day Regina invited my parents and me to her house for lunch. She must have been well over seventy, and she greeted us in black high heels and leopard-print tights. I couldn't stop staring at her outfit. I had never seen anyone so old dressed like that. She gave us a little tour of her living room. She showed us her collection of grand-father clocks and the portrait that Julio Romero de Torres had painted of her when she was an adolescent. Back then I had no idea who Romero de Torres was. In the portrait, Regina is posed with her mother, Serafina Longa, who had a rose cultivar named after her by a Bilbao botanist: the 'Serafina Longa'. Everything in the house was a curiosity or English. This is the backdrop of my father's big, fragmented novel: the vestiges of Neguri at the turn of the twentieth century, when the industries along the estuary were being built up and all the neighbours were trying to be British. It is also about the eighties, the decline of the neighbourhood, the shuttered factories, the problems of living in peace in the region, and about Regina Soltura, a *rara avis* nearing eighty, strolling around town in leopard-print tights and heels.

*

'Gabriela, in your book you can say that a man in a red ski mask got me out of bed at gunpoint,' he announced unexpectedly one day. I didn't answer. I didn't confess that I had put that in already, though I hadn't known the colour of the mask. 'Can I have Grandpa's war diary?' I asked after a while. My father stopped the car part way through a roundabout and said: 'That's my territory.'

XVIII

After my mother died I had a strange sense of well-being. During the autumn, I did whatever I felt like doing. I was sad, but I had no responsibilities: I was jobless, single and on leave from NYU.

In January I left Madrid and went back to New York to school and to look for work. Soon after I got to the city, my skin broke out and my hair turned oily. I couldn't get rid of the layers on the crown of my head. I went back to the university, to the office. I started to write about my mother, and to weigh each day against the same day the year before. Sometimes I caught a glimpse of myself from the outside and it was hard for me to recognise myself as the person who was working and going to class. I started to have dizzy spells, a queasiness that began in my head and descended to my stomach. The doctor said it was stress. The psychologist said I had lost my bearings and that to regain my balance I needed to make some changes in my life that scared me. The first step was to return to Madrid.

*

Wednesday, 19 December, 2012

I go out without washing my face, feeling the weight of dried tears in my eye sockets. Behind me are the river and

Manhattan, but I walk away from the towers, avoiding the sight of the city.

My last three hours in New York are spent at home, sitting on a box with a view of the skyline. I try to calculate the weight of the buildings. I count the windows and floors of a skyscraper and estimate what they must weigh, but neither my phone's calculator nor I can handle the load.

The place I'm about to leave has almost no walls or corners. Everything is glass and steel, and the city and the cold creep in past the steel and the glass. A few weeks after I moved in, I tried to warm up the space. I bought plants, throws and a few pieces of wooden furniture, but it didn't work. There was also the problem of the views. The constant presence of the city made it impossible to block out my surroundings. *I'm in New York, I'm in New York.* In the apartment, I was never able to forget that I lived in New York.

This morning was spent packing boxes, and as I packed them, I enjoyed watching the space clear bit by bit. When my mother saw it, the apartment was empty, and now I feel that it only makes sense that way. Diaphanous, with no obstacles between my memory and the skyline.

Tomorrow a removal company will come to pick up the boxes that are stacked in the living room. Someone will load them onto a cargo ship. The ship will sail down the river from Queens, cross the ocean and dock somewhere in the north of Spain, probably Vigo. In Vigo my boxes will be put on a truck that will cross the peninsula to Madrid. In Madrid the boxes will be unloaded in my new apartment.

I get into a black Lincoln from Northside Car Service. I tell the driver that I'm going to JFK. The driver is Latino and he asks me if I'm going to spend Christmas at home. I say yes. Then he asks me if I like soccer, and I say not much, but he doesn't seem to hear me, persisting: 'Are you for Real Madrid or Barça?' 'Neither,' I answer as I stare at the photograph on his licence. When we get on the BQE, the Empire State building comes into sight between the gravestones in the cemetery beneath the highway.

The black Lincoln stops in front of a little signpost for Iberia. The driver gets out, rolls up the sleeves of his jacket, and helps me unload my things. I thank him. I say: '*Feliz Navidad.*' The car drives away and I'm left alone with two suitcases and a rucksack.

XIX

RUNNING YOUR HAND OVER IT TO CALCULATE ITS
DIMENSIONS YOU THINK AT FIRST IT IS STONE THEN
INK OR BLACK WATER WHERE THE HAND SINKS IN
THEN A BOWL OF ELSEWHERE FROM WHICH YOU PULL
OUT NO HAND

ANNE CARSON, *The Beauty of the Husband*

Before my mother's death I lived as if the normal thing was to die of old age. I imagined my heart stopping on the eve of my hundred-and-first birthday, after an afternoon spent playing cards and dipping croissants in tea. I didn't think about death. Or not much. Now I believe that the standard is to die before one's time, like my grandfather Javier, like my mother, or like a friend of a friend who was hit by a car that ran a red light on the Castellana. An untimely death is always violent. Dying young is violent. Just as being shot is always untimely. No matter how old you are.

*

I find a photograph of my mother taken in the Atacama Desert. The file is called Death Valley and in the picture she's sitting against a wall of red rock. I also find something that I wrote about her in a notebook:

> After the death of a loved one, family and friends often look at pictures and pass them around to remember. Under the circumstances, the perception of the viewer is skewed. Nothing seems random; everything is a clue that reveals something about the causes of death.
>
> In the previous photograph, my mother is sitting at the foot of a rock wall in Chile's Death Valley. There are pictures of me in the same valley, but they will be irrelevant until I die.

*

Every time I think about my mother I remember her as vulnerable, though before her illness I doubt I saw her that way. This impression is a construct, created after the fact as my mind searched for early signs of her approaching death. Now, when I imagine her body, the first thing that comes to mind is the eczema that she had on her left hand, which she scratched constantly. I only really feared for her life once, when she had a separated placenta during the second month of pregnancy with my twin sisters. I was seven and we had come from Bilbao to Madrid to spend Christmas with my mother's parents. That day I watched as my great aunt carried a tangle of bloodstained sheets along my great-grandmother's hallway. It was just a few days before Christmas Eve and I thought it was a terrible time to be orphaned. My mother screamed as they moved her from the bedroom to the kitchen, her nightgown stained. Along the way she left a watery red trail that I followed until someone grabbed me and sat me in the living room between the television and my great-grandmother. The TV was on. A howl from the end of the hallway echoed through the china. I felt miserable and my unhappiness meshed with the commercials on TV: toothpaste, tomato sauce, Baby Feber dolls. I started to cry and my great-grandmother asked me to get her the box of sweets that she kept in the roll-top desk. My mother was taken out the back door so as not to soil the main staircase. I didn't see her go, but I imagined her being carried down the narrow stairs on a stretcher. I left the box of sweets on the table and went running to look at the stain on the mattress. I touched it and it was hot.

My mother was on bed rest for seven months. She couldn't move, because if she did either she or my sisters would die. My great aunt and I visited her every afternoon, and though her health was said to be improving, whenever I looked at her I saw a tangle of bloodstained sheets. It may be that the feeling of dread never left me. Now I'm convinced that every time I saw my mother in a nightgown, I was afraid that she was about to bleed to death and disappear.

XX

Last night I dreamed that I was in the back seat of a taxi on Calle Velázquez in Madrid. The car stopped at the traffic light on the corner of Calle Villanueva, in front of the entrance to the Hotel Wellington. I sat there for a while looking out the window at the gold braid on the doormen's jackets as I waited for the light to change. My phone rang and I reached into a cloth bag to retrieve it. At the other end of the line a woman said that she was going to kidnap me that night. I started to cry as she was talking. At the next light, the taxi seat turned into the yellow velvet sofa in the living room at home. I was still crying and moving in and out of the room as I packed my suitcase for the kidnapping. I folded some shirts that had been hanging to dry and I picked up a couple of notebooks. I imagined myself going mad in a hide-out and I cried even harder. I was terrified that I would lose my mind, and I planned to do exercises every day during my captivity: pacing from one end of my cell to the other, doing sit-ups. I imagined that there would be no bathroom and that I'd have to do my business in a corner. I saw myself going without food, smelling bad and doing push-ups on the floor. When I finished packing my suitcase I went out and walked to the door of the café where I'd agreed to meet the kidnapper. I woke up before she arrived.

On Facebook I find Kepa, a school friend from Getxo. I google his contacts and discover that several have been in prison. I see a picture of him with his arms around two guys who were in ETA. Kepa had a limp. One day he told me that at home they'd said he couldn't be my friend. He said that he had two cousins in jail. I managed to convince him that not talking was dumb and we talked until I moved to Madrid. Sometimes I wonder whether he ever thinks of me.

I find a video on YouTube of a man showing caches and explosives to a judge. They're in the middle of a forest. The man says:

We wanted to kidnap a Socialist councilman in Eibar.

I can't remember his name.

I can't remember where he lives, but I do know where he works.

He's the head of a school, a maths teacher.

We spent a few months shadowing him.

From October to December.

But in the end we gave up because he had a bodyguard.

I look at pictures of ETA commandos and I research their lives. I have a hard time coming to terms with them, because accepting their humanity means recognising that I'm capable of the same kind of things that they are. My mind was easier when I imagined that they were crazy or that they weren't people. Martians. Fiction.

*

El País, 17 February, 1981: 'Reactions to the Death of Joseba Arregui'. The forensic report acknowledges that the alleged ETA operative was tortured.

The presiding judge of Madrid's Trial Court Number 13, José Antonio de la Campa, presented a partial summary of the forensic report of the autopsy performed on Arregui. It confirms the existence of torture and physical violence. The cause of death was 'respiratory failure resulting from bronchopneumonia accompanied by severe pulmonary oedema'. The same judge took statements all afternoon from five officials of the Higher Police Force, part of the Regional Information Brigade, who participated directly in the interrogation.

> Santiago Brouard, president of HASI, the central political force of Herri Batasuna, and a doctor by profession, stated that the bronchopneumonia specified in the autopsy as present in the deceased was caused by the torture method known as *la bañera*, or bathtub, in which the person's head is submerged in a basin of dirty water, preventing him from breathing for a brief period. According to the Herri Batasuna leader, the torture victim is forced to swallow the contaminated liquid, which penetrates the lungs, causing bronchopneumonia.

El País, 9 March, 2009: 'Esteban Beltrán, human rights professor and director of Amnesty International, publishes the book *Twisted Rights*':

> No one sees torture as a problem in Spain, including the media. I provide examples of articles that go so far as to ask

'Does torture exist in Spain?' I don't know of any country in the world where there are no cases of torture and I believe that the role of the media is to investigate these cases. It would seem that the debate about torture has been appropriated by two camps: one, the Basque nationalist movement which claims that there is always torture, which isn't true; and the other, the government and everyone else, who claim that there is never torture and that there are sufficient safeguards against it. It's apparently not possible to say that ETA's crimes are terrible, that they must be denounced, and that those responsible for them must go to prison, but also that torture is a crime, and it must be investigated.

Website of the Psychiatric and Psychotherapeutic Research Institute of Madrid, Antonio Sánchez, 26 September, 2013: 'Trauma and Forgetting'.

In discussing denial and forgetting, it is especially relevant to cite the general attitude towards those who as children lived through a traumatic event; because of their youth, it is assumed that they aren't aware of what has happened to them, and at the same time they are presumed to be able to fully overcome the trauma, so that they are de facto denied the existence of the pain they experienced.

Email to my father from one of his cousins, 28 January, 2014:

I'm writing to you regarding the door of the Ybarra-Arregui mausoleum in the Derio cemetery. I believe I had mentioned that the bottom hinge is broken and now the door can't be opened all the way or locked.

I've found some metal workers through Vicenta, the woman who cleans the vaults. I met with them yesterday and they seem competent (and have good references).

It will cost something like €1000, but since the door has to be taken into the shop anyway, I'd like to have the sloppy old layers of paint stripped and a new coat applied (after the old paint is sandblasted). In other words, make it look nice and ready for the next hundred years. Painting the door would cost €300.

I've talked to my siblings and we think that the job could be split among the three families, not bothering with property shares. So you – the Ybarra Ybarras – would be responsible for payment of a third of the total, about €433.33. What do you say?

*

When my father hired his first security detail, I thought he didn't need it. In 2000, only politicians had bodyguards. We didn't want to see ourselves or him as a target. It was when he began to have protection that we realised we were being stalked by a terrorist group.

XXI

Friday, 28 March, 2014

'Gabriela, I need you to come to my office to pick up your mother's clothes. Choose the things you want to keep and take them. They're all over the place. I've been told there's a company that does pick-ups and delivers the clothes to churches. I'm going to phone them this week.' My father has been calling me for days with the same plea. I listen to it at a bus stop, sitting at my desk, in the car on the way home from a trip to the Pyrenees . . . Each time he sounds more desperate: 'Gabriela, when are you planning to come? Monday? Tuesday? What day is good for you?'

Before my father took my mother's clothes to his office, I intercepted the black dress that I wore to the burial. Between the funeral home and the various services, I had run out of dark things to wear and all I could think of was to look in my mother's cupboard. There were lots of dresses on the hangers, though hardly any of them were nice. She had long ago given up caring about her appearance and in recent years she bought only cheap things: clothes from beach stands, ugly shoes. My sisters and I used to laugh at her shoes. But the black dress was nice. Elegant. She had bought it in Italy. My sisters and I helped her choose it. We said: 'That one looks amazing on you,' and she wore it out of the store.

I've been putting off going through my mother's clothes for more than two years. Each time I think about doing it I imagine myself weeping over a heap of beach dresses and I postpone the trip. Today I decide that tomorrow I'll go. To prepare myself, I put on the black dress and head to a work meeting. On the way there on the Metro I imagine my mother in the same dark dress, her hips curvy.

I didn't wash the dress for a year. I didn't want it to lose her smell. But the day came when my sweat masked hers and I washed it. I touched the dress often, though I didn't put it on much. I never knew what shoes to wear it with. She wore it with horrible sandals with embroidered felt flowers. Tomorrow, I think, I'll look for them at my father's office. If she could wear them and not care, maybe I can too.

*

Monday, 31 March, 2014

I'm in my underwear in front of a pile of jackets. A little while ago I crossed Calle Mayor with a suitcase on the way to my father's office. The clothes that he wants to get rid of fill three cupboards. When I came into the office I set the suitcase in a corner, got undressed and began to try things on, checking to see how they looked in the mirror. Now I'm in the robe that my mother wore to breakfast every morning. The store where she bought it doesn't exist anymore. The fabric doesn't smell like her either; it smells like a mix of air freshener and mothballs. It isn't a nice day outside. It's raining in fits and starts. I try to remember, but it's hard. Many of the dresses don't say anything to me, and others bring back random moments: my mother in the kitchen stewing beans, my mother dressed to go out . . . There's a lot of noise from the street. I hear police sirens and megaphones. Official cars are everywhere. The people who get out of the cars are dressed in black and carry dark umbrellas. Next to the cathedral gates there are several reporters, cameras in hand. A thin girl in heels goes up the stairs. I open the suitcase and put in a blazer, a coat and a pair of blue trousers. I want to look out the window again. I'd like to think about my mother, sort through her clothes, write down what I remember . . . but I can't. All I can think about is turning to look outside again. It's Suarez's funeral. The president who was elected a few days after my grandfather was killed. There's a dark blue sedan parked at the gate. Mariano Rajoy came in it, I think. There are some old men leaning on their elbows on a wall. Like me, in my window.

XXII

Yesterday I told my father what my book was about. I told him that I wanted to go to Alto de Barazar to see the place where my grandfather was killed. 'I don't think you'll find anything there,' he said. 'It's just a forest.' At first I wanted him to come with me, drive up with me, help me search for the gully where the body was found, but when I suggested it, he said: 'I've been there already,' and I understood why he didn't want to come.

*

On the car trip from Madrid to Gorbea Natural Park it snowed, it rained and the sun came out. Some of the changes in weather were so swift and sudden that as I drove I had the sense of slipping in and out of the same dream. Snowy fields. Bare ground. Snowy fields. Bare ground. I've just parked the car under the canopy of an abandoned petrol station in Alto de Barazar to shelter from the hail. All that's left of the old petrol station is a rusty pump and a Gasoil sticker on one of the canopy pillars. To get here I followed the directions that the kidnappers sent the police: 'Cenauri-Vitoria highway. From Alto de Barazar, take the path that leads from the right side of the bar-restaurant'. The Cenauri-Vitoria highway is the N-240. Now I'm writing in the car. It's three o'clock. I'm facing the building that appears in the directions. It's an inn with an abandoned café, the walls yellowing and the shutters pulled down. Elgar's *Enigma Variations* is playing on the car radio. I imagine the Guardia Civil jeeps parked in the open space in front of the restaurant and on the other side of the motorway, where five snowploughs sit now.

*

I've reached the top of the trail that starts by the restaurant.

Before I started up, I put on a yellow raincoat and trainers. I walked around the building. The road that climbed through the trees was paved and I decided to drive up the mountain. Now I'm writing some more from the car. To my right there's a field with a big tree in the middle and a dozen sheep grazing around it. To my left is a path that heads into the forest.

I reach the pine grove where I think my grandfather was found: 'Trees grow very close together'. It's raining less. I'm writing with the notebook under my coat, but sometimes a drop falls on the zip and blots the page. I try to imagine the day when the body was found. I've seen photographs of the restaurant and the woods on the Internet and the place is familiar to me. Something like what happens when you visit the Empire State Building or the Eiffel Tower for the first time after having seen them many times on TV.

I take thirty steps down into the gully and I come to a small clearing littered with pine cones, ferns and branches. The clearing is covered in snow. This is the exact place where the kidnappers shot my grandfather, I think. I'm precisely thirty paces from the path. 'It is about thirty metres from the trail (RIP)'. The day that his body was found it was raining. It also rained all three days the police spent looking for his body. I imagine my grandfather standing and one of the kidnappers covering his face, putting the pistol to his temple and firing.

*

I'm back at the car. It's 4.04 p.m. The sheep are gone. The empty field makes me uneasy. A white SEAT is parked to my right, but I don't see anyone. It's starting to snow and I turn on the heat to warm my fingers. As I take notes I think about my grandfather, my mother and my father. About my mother telling us: 'Live lightly.' About my grandfather saying: 'The worst they can do is shoot me.'

*

To have a grave in the forest would be lovely. Perhaps I should hear the birds singing and the rustling above me. I would like such a thing as that.

ROBERT WALSER

Credits

Quotations from articles in *El País*, *ABC* and *Blanco y Negro* appear in the novel in slightly edited form. The same is true for the letters sent by the author's grandfather and uncles during the kidnapping, the instructions sent by ETA on how to find the body, and the excerpt from José Díaz Herrera's *Los mitos del nacionalismo vasco*. In the first part of the story, many passages are inspired by reports which appeared in the newspaper *El Correo Español—El Pueblo Vasco* between 21 May and 15 July 1977.

The excerpt from Antonio Machado's *Fields of Castile*, translated by Stanley Appelbaum, is reprinted with the permission of Dover Publications Inc. Passages from Robert Walser's *The Walk*, translated by Christopher Middleton with Susan Bernofsky, are reprinted with the permission of New Directions Publishing Corp., © New Directions, 2012, and the excerpt from Anne Carson's *The Beauty of the Husband* is reprinted with the permission of Anne Carson and Jonathan Cape, © Anne Carson, 2001. The image of Robert Walser lying dead in the snow is reproduced with the permission of Keystone and the Robert Walser Foundation, and the photographs of the author's father in handcuffs are reproduced with the permission of the *ABC* archive.

Acknowledgements

To Enrique, Inés and Leticia. To my first readers: Álvaro, Beatriz, Blanca, Iñaki, Mireya and Sonia. To Mónica and Ignacio for lending me their car to drive up to Alto de Barazar. To my editors, Elvira Navarro and Ellie Steel. To my translator, Natasha Wimmer. To Carlos.

In memory of my mother, my grandparents and Roque, one of my best friends, who died in the capital of Angola on 12 October 2012. The last time we saw each other we had dinner at a restaurant on Callejón de Puigcerdá and I told him the plot of this novel.